30 LOVE

A NOVEL

RAN WALKER

10 9 8 7 6 5 4 3 2 1

ISBN 9781020001055

45 Alternate Press, LLC
Hampton, Virginia

1

___

I'm not totally sure, but I sense that our parents intended for us to be twins. Lailah and I were born on the same day in the same hospital, while our parents, who've been best friends since childhood, anxiously awaited our arrivals. Lailah came first, beating me into this world by nearly two hours, but to her credit, she's never held this over my head.

Because our mothers picked out our names, we were nearly given the same one. My name is Dominic Parker, and Lailah's full name is Dominique Lailah Landfair. Thank goodness our fathers intervened and suggested that we each be called by other names, for the sake of avoiding confusion, because if our mothers had had their way, the only distinction in the pronunciation of our two names would have been whether a person chose to emphasize the "ih" sound in my name, as opposed to the "ee" sound in hers. Instead, I got the nickname of Dizzy, which my father gave me because he said I had these huge cheeks (plus, pops is a serious jazz aficionado), and Lailah's parents started calling her by her middle name. One would think they could have just given us different names, rather than complicate the situation.

An even more interesting tidbit is that Lailah and I have been having joint birthday parties ever since we were three years old, just like real twins. At first our parents tried to throw us our own individual parties at different times on the same day, but according to my mother, all I could do was talk about Lailah's party, with no interest whatsoever in my own, and to hear Lailah's mom tell it, it was the same way on her end, as well. We ended up sharing our birthday parties up until we graduated from Daily High School. From there, things changed a bit.

We both ended up moving from Daily, Mississippi, to Atlanta, Georgia, for college, although we ended up at different institutions. From there, we tried celebrating our birthday together freshman year, but after that, it seemed that the idea of doing such a thing had already run its course. It wasn't until this year that I suggested to Lailah that we restore our old ritual and go out to dinner to celebrate our thirtieth birthday. She agreed without fanfare.

I guess if she had better options, she probably would have exercised them.

❦

IT'S EASY TO THINK THAT A BOY AND A GIRL WHO had spent so much time around each other would have naturally gone the way of *Love and Basketball* and *Brown Sugar* by trying to hook up at some point. I was definitely down with the idea, but apparently Lailah wasn't. I can't lie, though. I have had a crush on her since we started kindergarten, although I never hinted at it until we were in the eleventh grade.

I remember leaning against my battered old Honda Accord, trying to keep warm, while my nerves buzzed so hard that I thought I was going to pass out. I had been hinting at my feelings for weeks using a variety of different methods, but that particular day, with all of my earlier attempts having failed, I couldn't take it any more. I broke down and spilled my guts on why I thought we should be together.

She didn't look as surprised as I thought she would be, but her words were distant and calculated, nonetheless. "Dizzy, you're my best friend. Best *friend*," she emphasized. "If we start dating and it doesn't work out, then where will that leave us? I want to always have you in my life, and the only way to guarantee that is not to complicate things."

I was floored by her comments. I even rationalized against what she was saying.

"We're just taking our friendship to a new level. That's all. We won't stop being friends just because we open this new door and walk through it."

Then she used the words that caused me to acquiesce: "I love you, and I want to always have you in my life. I value you more than having you as just my boyfriend."

All I could hear was "I love you," and I was happy just hearing that part. From that point forward, I never pushed the issue. Just knowing that she loved me was enough for me to not rock the boat.

❦

WHILE I WAS AT ELLISON-WRIGHT COLLEGE and she was over at Georgia State University, we had a solitary moment that tested this idea of us just being friends and nothing more. It was during our junior years, shortly after Ellison-Wright's homecoming game, and Lailah had just come out of a bad relationship two weeks earlier (I had been single since the beginning of the semester). She was pretty heartbroken and wrestling with whether or not she should forgive her ex-boyfriend for cheating on her with a girl who had just crossed into his sister sorority. Halfway through our conversation, she decided to take a shower, so I just sat on the bed in her room, waiting for her to return.

When she finally came through the door fifteen minutes later, her petite caramel complexion wrapped in a large beach towel, droplets of water still peppering her shoulders and legs, my jaw dropped. When she saw my reaction, she smiled.

"Dayum!" I said, not even attempting to avert my eyes. I didn't feel that there was a reason to, especially since it was no secret that I was attracted to her and had been harboring suppressed feelings for quite a few years.

"You've never seen me naked, have you?" she asked casually.

"Not like this. All grown up."

"Remember when we used to play behind your

house and you would show me yours and I would show you mine?"

I couldn't pull the memory to mind, but I nodded anyway.

"There have been times that I wondered what you looked like naked," she said.

I couldn't tell if she was just teasing me or if she was trying to get it on and poppin' in that room.

"All you have to do is just ask," I said.

"We definitely don't need to open that door."

"Okay, but if we're as close as you say we are, you should be able to walk around naked in front of me."

I was just saying something to be coy, but when she faced me, unwrapped her towel, and dropped it to the floor, standing before me completely naked, I was speechless. My eyes went straight to her firm breasts and silver dollar-sized chocolate areolas, nipples growing erect in the cool room. I scanned down her lean frame to the trimmed upside down triangle of hair that rested atop the intersection of her thighs. And just as soon as she revealed herself to me, she reached for a large t-shirt and pulled it down over herself, covering up all of the treasures I had just laid my eyes upon.

"Whoa!" I said. "Back track. Pon de replay! Let me see that again!"

"Once is enough," she said, with a smirk on her face, clearly satisfied by my expression.

I tried again to negotiate, sounding almost like a little kid in the process. "Please show me again. Just one more time!"

She laughed. "You're funny."

Turning on the television atop her dresser, she

walked over to the bed I was sitting on and lay down next to me. "Can you rub my back?"

"Sure," I responded.

I reached over and grabbed some lotion from her dresser, moistened my hands, and then slowly eased them over her sexy ass onto her lower back. In the back of my mind, I felt that if I did her back right, she might let me massage a bit more of her. As she lay there with my hands sweeping softly across her shoulder blades and onto the muscles on either side of her backbone, she talked about how being alone sucked, about how relationships were never what they were supposed to be, and about how what we had was the purest form of love that she believed she could experience.

"Maybe we should get together romantically," I said, careful to make it sound like I was only proposing something that was logical and not necessarily emotionally based.

"I can't lie and say that I haven't thought about it, but I don't want to be lying here again on some night in the future, feeling the pain that I'm feeling right now, and not have anyone to comfort me and tell me that everything is going to be okay. You can't be both things to me, and I don't want to lose your friendship, so I think we should keep things the way they are."

I sighed, but continued to knead the muscles in her back. "But what if you never meet a man as good for you as I am? Be honest. We get each other more than anyone else possibly could. I think the longer we play this game, the more time we're gonna waste."

"I'm sure you'll graduate and find the perfect

woman who will be all of those things that you think you see in me. We won't even be having this conversation five years from now."

That's when I said it: "I'll make a deal with you. If we're both single and have no potential prospects on the horizon when we turn thirty, then we should marry each other."

She slid away from my hands and sat up on the bed. "I seriously doubt that either of us will be single by the time we're thirty. That's *ten* years. A lot can happen in all of that time."

"That's all the more reason to agree to it then. I'm serious. If we've made it that far in our lives and both come up empty-handed, then that would be proof positive that we're supposed to be together."

She sat quietly, pondering this.

"I don't want to be old when I start a family," I added. "And from what you've told me, you don't either."

I sat watching her, wondering what she was thinking, and then she slowly leaned over and kissed me softly on the lips. It was simple, and might have even been platonic, but it was amazing all the same. Looking directly into my eyes, she said, "If we're still available by the time we turn thirty, I will definitely marry you."

I remember feeling a glow overtake my body—even though the likelihood of our getting married was so remote that I figured there would be a black president of the United States before such a thing occurred.

As if to yank a little bit of the wind from my sails, she added, "I don't plan on being single when I turn thirty, though."

§

THAT WAS ALL TEN YEARS AGO, AND I'M NOT sure if Lailah even remembers it. I would like to believe that she does and that I'm not the only one who has replayed what happened that night at various points throughout these past ten years. So tonight after dinner, I will propose to her. I'm open to the possibility of a life with her (and always have been), but I realize that it takes two for that.

We will just have to see what happens.

2

———

$\mathscr{I}$ had originally planned on doing something far more elaborate for my proposal, but when I considered that there was a looming possibility she would say "no," I cowered and opted for something that was ninety-five percent more low key.

I drive by her house around 6:30 on Thursday evening, wearing a pair of dark jeans, a white button-up, and a navy blue blazer. As soon as she lets me in, she comments on how I'm dressed.

"You must have something special planned tonight," she says, smiling and looking me up and down.

"Can't a brotha throw on a coat to take his best friend out for her birthday? I was trying not to look like a damn jheri curl baybo up in this piece."

She laughs, placing her hand against my chest. I love it when she does that.

"Well, do I need to change then?" she asks, pointing to her ribbed tank-top, tight jeans, and a pair of stylish wine colored heels that match her purse.

"You look good to me. Plus, it's your birthday! Wear what the hell you want to wear."

"It's your birthday, too, Dizzy! I don't even know why I expected you to come by here looking more casual, maybe wearing a t-shirt and a pair of Jordans."

"Well, these are Cole Haan with Nike Air soles," I say, modeling the shoe as if I'm a sales rep for Nike. "Comfort and style!"

She laughs, reaching for her purse. "As long as you don't have me walking all over Atlanta tonight, I should be okay in these."

"Nice pedicure."

"You know a sister couldn't go out on her birthday without getting her toe game straight."

"You actually have very nice feet," I say. This comment is not original to our conversations, but I know she can appreciate it more now that she is preparing to strut through the city.

"Thanks," she responds. "I'm thinking about getting a tattoo on top of my foot."

"A tattoo of what?"

"I'm thinking a lotus or something like that."

"One of those Buddhist things, I'm guessing."

She smiles. "You should try it sometime. Maybe you wouldn't be so stressed."

"I'm working on it. Maybe if I found the right woman I wouldn't be so stressed."

I toss out the comment as a hint—a bit of fore-shadowing, if you will. She just touches my chest again and grabs her purse.

We hop in my Jeep Wrangler, which I'm very thankful hasn't given me any problems this month. I open the door for her, and in spite of her heels, she hops up into the vehicle with hardly any effort, leaning over to crack open my door for me.

"Ready to kick off number thirty?" I ask.

"It's kind of funny, isn't it? I mean, who would think that we'd still be celebrating our birthdays together after all of these years."

"That's not a bad thing. In fact, I can't think of any other way that I'd rather spend it."

"You're sweet," she says. "Now let's go and grab dinner. A sista is starting to get hungry!"

LAILAH HAD MADE RESERVATIONS AT HOUSTON'S, her favorite restaurant in Buckhead. It's a place that I don't eat at unless I'm with her. I prefer that rather nice assortment of wings offered by more Southwest Atlanta establishments like J. R. Crickets. I figure for the price of a meal at Houston's I can get a whole heap of wings, fries, and drinks—plus a perfect view of whatever game is playing on the giant HD LED screens hanging around the restaurant. It's paradise for a guy like me, but it's not surprising that Houston's won out tonight, though. I don't think that Lailah would have ever forgiven me if I made her eat wings for her birthday and she ended up getting wing sauce on her clothes.

Thank goodness for the reservation, because without it, we would be at the end of a very long waiting list—which is a bit surprising to me since it's a Thursday.

We are seated at a dimly lit booth in the back of the restaurant, and there are more than enough young professionals in here. I look down at my clothing and realize that I have accidentally put on the official uniform for single black men. Now I wish I had opted for the Jordans, just so that I wouldn't look like another one of the buppie clones in here.

Lailah orders a filet mignon medium, and I order a well-done Ahi Tuna plate.

"Why do you like your steaks bloody?" I ask, messing with her.

"Medium is pink, not bloody. What you're talking about is rare."

"You know what I mean."

"Are you serious? Don't tell me you're the kind of brotha who would ruin a fine cut of beef by over-cooking it!"

"Don't make this about me," I say, laughing. "This is about you eating pink meat. Now don't get me wrong, I'll eat pink meat, but not steak."

"Dang, Dizzy!" Lailah squeals. "You are so crass!"

One of the perks of having known a person for your entire life is that you have a wide and complete understanding of the other person's personality and you're able to laugh off what might otherwise offend anyone else.

"Goony goo-goo!" I say playfully.

"Goony goo-goo, boo boo," she responds, plucking my wrist with her nicely manicured nails.

"I'm convinced that we're the only people who will ever get us."

"Maybe," she says, chuckling. "Remember back when we were little and we had an entire language worked out?"

"Yeah. I still can't believe we could stretch that Eddie Murphy joke so far."

"Well, we were creative back then."

"Back then?" I say. "We're still creative now, Miss Writer Extraordinaire."

She smiles, lifting her glass of white zinfandel. "Well, let's toast to it then. To remaining creative in this thirtieth year of life!"

"Well, actually it will be our thirty-first year when you really think about it, since we lived a year before we turned one."

"Dizzy, you're such a nerd!"

"But you love me."

"Yes, I do. To a great thirty-first year of life," she says, clinking my glass.

She has no idea of how great I want it to be, though.

❧

AFTER WE FINISH DINNER, I ASK LAILAH IF there's anything that she would like to do. She just says she's along for the ride. For a while I just drive along Peachtree Street before turning off the strip towards Ellison-Wright College. When we pull up on campus, she leans forward.

"Why are we stopping here?"

"I figure we could go for a little walk and just kick back and chill."

"Okay."

She could easily put up a struggle if she wanted, but she doesn't, and there's a part of me that wonders if she knows what I am planning to do. I had been subtly dropping hints already, so if she has made the connection already, then that would be cool because it would mean that she was already on board. But then I'm assuming that she actually remembers a single conversation that occurred once, roughly ten years ago.

As we walk onto the campus, the night sky is blanketed with so many stars that it feels like we are inspiring a new constellation above our heads. Even the moon, glowing like the tip of a fingernail, casts the perfect glow. The scene feels very romantic, especially since there are hardly any students ambling about the campus.

"How are your mom and dad?" she asks.

"Same ole same ole. Dad claims that he's trying to cut back on his practice, but I don't think he knows how. And Mom just started taking French at the local community center. I'm thinking she's trying to con him into taking her to Paris soon."

Lailah smiles. "They should do that. Go to Paris. That would be so romantic."

"Yeah," I offer. I start to say, "Maybe you and I should go to Paris," but I'm starting to feel the butterflies building up on me, so I just let the moment pass.

She reaches down and takes off her shoes.

"You sure you want to walk barefoot around here?"

"At this point, I don't care. My feet are killing me!"

"Well, hop on my back."

"Seriously?"

"Seriously."

I crouch down and Lailah straddles my back. I hoist her up onto my back, cuffing my arms beneath the backs of her knees. Her shoes bounce off of my left shoulder as she holds them, trying to keep them out of my face.

"Let me know when I get too heavy."

"Girl, I could carry you all day," I lie.

I walk us around the campus square and stop at the administration building steps, sitting her down.

"We can chill here, if you don't mind," I say.

This is the spot I have selected for the proposal. I figured I should do it on the stairs so that she wouldn't immediately notice I was kneeling already. My nerves are starting to get the better of me, though.

"What's wrong?" she asks.

"What do you mean?"

"Something's not right."

"What makes you say that?"

She rolls her eyes. "I know you better than anyone else in the world. Of course I'm going to notice when you have something weighing on your mind."

I decide to roll with her conversation.

"You're right. You do know me better than anyone else on the planet, so I'm curious if you can look into my eyes right now and tell me what I'm thinking."

I can tell that she likes the challenge because she leans forward attentively, setting her gaze on me with an intensity that she tends to reserve for when she's in her ultra-writing mode. "Okay."

As she looks at me, I try to project all of my thoughts through my eyes. I even start to amplify my thoughts, in hopes that she might be able to tune into the vibrations of my soul. I begin to confess how much she means to me as telepathically as I can. Who knows? Maybe she and I are connected in such a way that anything is possible. If we are, I wouldn't be surprised.

"There's something you want to tell me," she eventually says.

I don't know if she's fishing for information or if she is really cracking through the layers of my mind.

She turns her head, looking at me quizzically. "It involves me, too."

I don't nod or smile. It takes everything to keep a straight face and let her finish chipping away at me.

"It has something to do with us—turning thirty," she adds.

She is so hot that I almost blurt out everything, but I hold tight, anxious to hear what she will say next.

"You're appreciative of our friendship," she says.

She is starting to cool off now. I want to nudge her back towards my thoughts, hoping not to lose this connection that I think we're sharing.

As if she's reading my thoughts, she comes back to the subject of our thirtieth birthday. "There's something important about this birthday," she says. I can feel in her voice that she's starting to reach a little. She wants me to give her a sign, but I sit quietly, continuing to engage her gaze.

"Yeah," she says. "You want to tell me something important, and it's connected with our thirtieth birthday." As she closes her mouth, she sits back against the steps. She's done what she can do, and this is where I'm supposed to come in and fill in the blanks.

I finally allow my lips to curl into a smile, and she smiles in return.

"You do have something to tell me," she says. "Go ahead."

I am already in a kneeling position, facing her on the stairs, but the positioning of my body is inconspicuous, as far as I can tell.

"Well, I do have something to tell you. And it *is* connected to our turning thirty."

She nods her head, urging me on.

"You have always been my best friend, and I have cherished our friendship from the moment I even knew what a friend was. You are my oldest and dearest friend in the world."

"I'm the same age as you," she says.

"What do you mean?" Her comment slides right over my head, and my heart starts beating even faster.

"You said that I'm your oldest friend. I'm sure you have friends who are older than thirty!"

"Oh, yeah. You know what I mean," I say, stumbling to recover.

"I'm sorry, Dizzy. I didn't mean to interrupt you. Keep going, baby."

I feign being flustered. "You got me all discombobulated and shit."

She laughs, and I feel the butterflies begin to swell even further.

"Okay," I continue. "I have known you ever since you used to wear Afro puffs and suck your thumb like a Monchichi."

She nudges me playfully.

"I have been spoiled by your beauty, both inner and outer, for these past thirty years, and you have taught me what it means to love someone unconditionally."

Her look is now serious, and I wonder if she can see where all of this is headed. Rather than try to keep her in suspense, I push forward toward the grand finale.

"I don't know if you remember this, but ten years ago we were in your dorm room and you had just come out of a bad relationship. It was homecoming weekend over here, but I knew you were going through it, so I went over to see you at Georgia State. That night we talked about a lot things, and we even made a promise to each other. We said that if we were both single when we turned thirty..."

Lailah's eyes widen and her posture stiffens. "Oh my god, oh my god!" she says.

I can't tell if that's a good thing or a bad thing. In all of the years that I've known her, I've never seen her look like this. It's a half-crazed look, and I wonder if this is the look right before she explodes in euphoria or if it's the look that precedes the ultimate destruction of the longest friendship I've ever known.

I plow ahead, since the door is already open.

Reaching into my back pocket, I pull out a small costume ring, one that resembles the Cracker Jack ring I gave her when we were little kids playing "husband and wife." (She would make me propose to her before she would let me kiss her cheek and pretend to be her husband.)

"Cracker Jack doesn't make rings anymore, but I found this one at an antique shop. It's just a placeholder and a reminder that I have loved you for a very long time."

Lailah's eyes are now beginning to glass over, and I take her hand.

"I believe that we were made for each other, and just like I said ten years ago, I feel our being single in the world right now is proof positive that we were destined to be together. I love you more than I have ever loved anyone, so I am asking you right here and right now, under this beautiful sky, on this night, our thirtieth birthday, if you will do me the honor of being my wife."

Her hand tightens around mine, and tears trickle out onto her cheeks. I can feel her response coming, and my heart is racing a mile a minute.

With her free hand she wipes her eyes. Time freezes as I await her response.

"I love you," she finally says.

I feel a relief flood throughout my system, as if the sunshine has sailed halfway around the earth just to dance inside of me at this moment. "I love you, too," I say.

"I love you," she says again. "But I can't marry you."

3

I can scarcely remember the drive to Lailah's house, and in the days since our birthday, I haven't heard from her. I've texted her repeatedly and left messages on her voicemail, but she's gone completely off the grid. It's been almost a week, and I'm starting to sense that I might have made an irreparable mistake proposing to my best friend. What was I thinking? I should have just left well enough alone.

I have been trying to keep myself busy with work so that I wouldn't notice her absence, but that's been next to impossible. I have even considered going out for drinks with some of the folks from work, but I'm afraid that I might actually run into Lailah, and that would make for an awkward situation that I don't think either of us is ready to handle just yet. Mostly I just come home, open my laptop, and watch this new creepy show I discovered on the FX Network called *American Horror Story*. Either that or read one of the many sci-fi novels that have been collecting dust on my bookshelves since Lailah gave me an e-book reader two Christmases ago.

(Picking up that device now makes me think too much of her, so I'm back to dead trees for the time being.) The only thing I have to do now is stop the incessant urge to check my phone, e-mail, and Facebook messages to see if she's decided to reach out to me.

This situation is really killing me.

It would be strange if it all ended here, if our thirty years of friendship just evaporated into nothingness. Before I returned to Atlanta from New York, four years had passed since I had last seen her. We had talked on the phone, but she hadn't made the trip up to see me, and I hadn't made the trip down to see her.

In those days I was on the grind trying to make something happen in Silicon Alley. Coming from the background of a college English major, it took me a while to get myself into the tech industry. In those days, I was doing some independent contracting work as a technical writer, scribbling instructions for products that the average person would probably never use. After a while, I was able to network with a few game developers who were looking for someone to help design and develop storylines for their games. That's what I've been doing ever since, and I love it with a passion.

Leaving New York wasn't even my idea, but to cut costs, the team felt we could move to Atlanta and begin angling ourselves to do app development for these new cell phone operating systems. By the time we made it here, the iPhone and Android platforms were catching on fire. The irony is that while we have been doing game development for quite some time, a number of other developers just popped out of thin air with the simplest of ideas and graphics to make what are now being heralded as the highest grossing games of the year. Too much Faulkner and Ellison apparently destroyed my ability to create a game as simple as *Angry Birds*. Go figure.

Even though my company, JACOPLEX, brought me here, the thought of catching up with Lailah was the icing on the cake. I missed her so much that I wasted no time in reconnecting with her when I returned. We started spending more time together than we had even spent when we were in college. Truthfully, it felt like we were in high school again, hanging out at least once a week (if not more). She would talk about her job, some random bozo she was dating, and where she wanted to be before she turned forty. Marriage never came up, but I sensed that she just hadn't been in a situation where that was even an option. Instead, she had focused her attention on becoming one of those Forty Under Forty people that magazines credit with being the next generation of leaders. And she is well on her way, having written several novels that have won all kinds of awards. She keeps talking about positioning herself for the MacArthur Foundation "Genius" Grant, and I'm hopeful that she eventually gets what she wants. If I could give her my own Pulitzer Prize for fiction or poetry or whatever it is that she decides to write, I would award it to her every year.

With all of the emptiness of the past few days, I have considered whether or not I should try on a new hobby for size, but honestly speaking, there's no substitute for the quality time I was spending with Lailah. If nothing happens soon, I don't know if I'll ever be able to fully recover from what I did.

WHILE IN THE MIDDLE OF THE LATEST EPISODE of *American Horror Story*, I feel my phone vibrating. I grab it, praying that it's Lailah finally putting an end to this madness. When I check the caller ID, I see that it's her friend Marcia. I quickly answer it. I know that Lailah has probably been talking to Marcia, so Marcia is going to be the only person right now who can tell me what the hell is going on.

"Hello?"

"Hey, Dizzy. Are you busy?"

"Not at all."

"Can you meet me at the food court at Phipps Plaza in an hour?"

I don't even hesitate. "Yes."

"Okay. See you then."

Then she hangs up, and I'm left holding the phone with a million thoughts swirling around inside of my head. I'm assuming that this all has to do with Lailah, but I never got a chance to ask. I shake my head. Yes, this is about Lailah, because Marcia's not the kind of person to push up on her girl's best friend.

I grab a baseball cap and toss on a windbreaker. The drive will take a little over half an hour, and it takes everything in me to keep my thoughts from blinding me along the way.

When I arrive at Phipps, I immediately head for the food court. I'm there for nearly forty minutes before I see Marcia come up the escalator. She has her weave pulled back into a ponytail. It looks almost natural, but I can still tell it's a weave—mainly because she is the self-proclaimed queen of weaves.

I wave so she can see me. I rise from my seat and give her a hug.

"Dizzy, Dizzy, Dizzy," she starts, as she sits down at the small circular table.

"I'm sweating bullets over here, Marcia. Don't play. Please tell me something. She's not even taking my calls."

"Dude, you really came out of left field on her, didn't you?"

"We made a promise to each other. I just felt it was time to follow through."

"No warning or nothing? Boy, you're a bold one."

"It's hardly a secret that I've been feeling her forever."

"Let me ask you this: did you actually expect for her to say 'yes'?" Marcia asks.

"I don't know what I was thinking. But I felt for a moment that she was gonna accept. How's she doing? Is she okay?"

"She's a'ight. She's just been playing through all of this stuff in her head."

"What stuff? Is she still considering it?"

Marcia leans in closer. "I'm not supposed to be telling you any of this stuff, because she's my girl and all, but on the real, I think the two of you would be adorable together."

"So what did she tell you?" I ask. I am completely on pins and needles now.

"She called me as soon as she got home, and she went on for the next three hours about what you did. I told her that she should be calling you and telling you all of this stuff, but I'm not sure that she really knew what she wanted to say. Needless to say, she's been talking about you all week, going back and forth between being mad at you for putting her on the spot and wondering what it would be like if the two of you actually hooked up."

I can feel my heart starting to race with excitement, but I'm afraid to let myself get too worked up. I'm just glad that I have been on Lailah's mind.

Marcia continues, "So every day this week your girl has been talking my ear off. Dizzy this, Dizzy that. I told her that she needed to just call you and stop using up all the minutes on my cell phone."

I smile when I hear "your girl."

"What should I do then?" I ask. "I don't want to put any more pressure on her."

"I remember a few years back when La was dating some jerk who was just toying with her feelings and how you had her back and gave her a shoulder to cry on. As far as I could tell, you were a pretty cool guy for being there for her like that. She even told me how you offered to go put a beat down on the dude, but how she talked you out of it. I even asked her later on why she never tried to get at *you*, since it seemed like she was using you as the standard for who she dated anyway. She said that it wasn't like she didn't want to. She was just afraid to mess up the friendship you two had. And now look at you two. On the verge of something and nothing at the same time."

"So should I let it go or push on?" I ask.

"I just need to know if you're serious about this thing. I think that's the thing she's most worried about—like this might be a game to you or something. I mean, have you really thought about what it means to be married? Because if all of this is just about some promise you made when you two were still kids, there's no point in getting her all worked up like this."

I look into Marcia's eyes. "I love her. Seriously. And I always hoped we would get married one day. Dominic and Dominique, you know."

"Well, I already told you what I think. Y'all are two peas in a pod anyway."

"So what should I do then?"

"Have you tried calling her?"

"Yeah, she won't answer or call me back."

"I figured," she says, pondering the situation. "I tell you what. Just trail me over to her house."

She can probably tell by my reaction that I'm confused as hell by her suggestion.

"You love her, right?"

"No doubt."

"Well, I know she'll answer the door for me. You just make sure you're standing there when she does."

WHEN LAILAH ANSWERS THE DOOR, MARCIA immediately says, "I brought someone over here with me."

"Oh girl!" Lailah responds when she sees me step into view.

"Y'all need to talk to each other and not around each other. I'm out of here. Call me next week, girl!" Marcia says over her shoulder as she returns to her car.

Now Lailah and I are standing alone at the door, facing each other. She looks disheveled, but beautiful. I can tell she's been vegging out because her

curly hair is flying in every direction and she's
wearing a large t-shirt that falls low on her thighs,
just above the tights she's wearing.

"Are you going to invite me in?" I finally ask.

"Come in."

As I step into the foyer of her two-level suburban
tract house, I admire the tranquil vibe. There's some
heavy feng shui shit going on up in here.

"I can't believe she just brought you over here
like that," she says, leading me to the couch in
the den.

"You wouldn't take my calls or get back
with me."

"Don't take it personal. I've just been thinking.
You know how I get when I get inside my head. I
can get lost in there."

"I've been lost in my own head, too. I was
praying like hell that I hadn't lost you after what I
said."

She closes her eyes for a moment, as if preparing
her thoughts. When she opens them, she angles her
body toward mine.

"What was the other night about?" she finally
says.

"It was about me trying, for once, to tell you
what I wanted out of our friendship."

"So you really want to marry me?" she asks. "Is
that even possible, given that we've never even
dated?"

"Anything is possible. And as far as I'm concerned, our relationship is above dating anyway.
Dating is what people do when they are trying to get
to know each other. We know each other already."

"Not intimately."

"We can always work that out," I say coyly.

She doesn't give me her usual smile. "I'm still tripping that you asked me."

"I told you that I would ten years ago."

"Dizzy, people say all kinds of shit when they're young. I was convinced I would marry Brian McKnight one day."

"Stop lying, La. You know you had a thing for Stoney Jackson."

"Boy, I don't do jheri curls."

"Well, that rules out half the niggas in Memphis."

At this, she finally laughs, and I am so relieved that all I want to do is bask in her laughter for the next few minutes.

"Seriously, while you were pining over Brian, I was trying to keep from letting you know that you were my number one."

"Oh, so you never had a celebrity crush?"

"Well, there was Janet."

She smiles. "Why do all guys want to get with Janet Jackson?"

"I didn't say Janet Jackson. I'm talking about Janet Jacme."

"Who?"

"She's a porn star."

Lailah shakes her head. "I should have known."

"But she doesn't hold a candle to you," I add with a smile.

"I hope not," she responds, chuckling.

I take her hand, and she allows me to hold it.

"See, this is why I know we're made for each other. We're the only ones who really get us."

"But is that enough of a reason to get married?

Marriage is serious. It's not just a ceremony. It's a lifetime together."

"I know. I would still want you—even if you looked like you just rolled out of bed with your hair sticking up all over your head like Who Shot John and Why."

She touches her hair. "Oh shit!" she says, jumping off the couch and running for the bathroom down the hall.

"Don't worry," I call out. "You don't have to get all Scott Pilgrim on me. I love the natural look."

I can hear her laughing, and she returns moments later with a long-billed baseball cap pulled low on her head.

"No, take that thing off. You're too beautiful to be rocking something that fugly."

"I'm not taking it off, so you'll have to just get used to it, pal."

"Fair enough."

She looks at me for a moment, her eyes barely visible beneath the brim of the hat. "I don't know about all of this, Dizzy."

"Just answer one question for me. Do you love me?"

"Yes, but I don't know if it's the same way that you say you love me."

I chew on my bottom lip for a moment. "So you're saying you're not attracted to me?"

"I *am* attracted to you."

"Well, are you saying that you can't view me as your man?"

"I'm not exactly saying that either."

"Well, what are you saying then?"

Lailah lowers her head and stares at her toes. "I don't know what I'm saying, man."

"Just tell me how you really feel. That's the only way we'll know which direction we need to take things."

She looks up slowly and stares at me for what seems like an eternity. I can't make out her thoughts. After all, I did just pop up here unannounced and put all of this stuff in her face while I stood by waiting for her response.

She leans toward me, and I see her eyes beginning to close, so I lean forward, quickly kissing her. Her lips are soft as they press against mine, and I all I want is to stay with her in this moment. When she pulls away, I have no idea of what she is thinking.

"You know all of this is crazy, right?" she says.

"Yeah, but if you're gonna do something crazy, you should do it with me. In the whole scope of things, this is just an extension of the crazy things that we've already done in our lives."

She ponders this for a moment. "So you are serious about all of this then?"

"Dead serious."

"Will you always love me and want me?"

"Definitely."

"Will you still be in love with me if I gain fifty pounds or I lose my arm in an accident or something?"

"Yes—and why are you asking me all of this?"

She takes my hand. "Because in marriage, people change and things happen. I don't ever want to get divorced, so I just need to know that what you're telling me is a commitment you can make for the rest of your life."

I lift her hand to my lips and kiss it softly. "I want to get old with you."

She smiles before leaning in and kissing me again. This kiss is even softer and nicer than the first. When she pulls away this time, she tosses that ugly ass baseball cap onto the floor.

"Okay, Dizzy. Let's do it."

4

Only after I've had a chance to get a good night's sleep does the magnitude of what we're doing truly sink in. Somehow the word "marriage" feels different than it did yesterday. Before, it was something I was aspiring to, but now it is something I'm about to actually do.

I look around my apartment and realize at some point in the not-so-distant future I will be sharing all of the stuff in here: the Star Wars posters, the electric guitar I bought just because the shit looked cool (even though I never learned to play a lick), my funky ass futon (if that thing could talk, oh my god!), my original Macintosh computer case (which is empty, but serves as an insanely great paper weight), and a baseball cap collection that would put Mr. Marcus to shame. In all honesty, she'll probably push to get rid of some of this stuff—especially the futon. I might have to fight for the other stuff though.

What's of even greater concern now is that we have to let everyone else in on our plans, including our parents. I have no freaking idea of what they're going to say. Truthfully, I wasn't convinced that Lailah would even say "yes," so the notion of actually calling her parents in advance to talk about the proposal didn't make much sense to me. I figured if she said "no" then no one would have to ever know about this hiccup in our friendship. Now, I have to not only tell *my* parents about all of this, but I also need to talk to her parents first. Before I left her house last night, I told her to keep everything under wraps until I could get Mr. Landfair and Mrs. Landfair's permission. She thought that was such a gentleman's gesture, but I know the Landfairs and I know my parents, and all of them are old school and don't play that neo-styled cowboy shit where a guy ducks and dodges the family until the wedding. Granted some things about Mississippi have changed through the years, that isn't one of them.

The more I think about calling Mr. and Mrs. Landfair, the more I realize that's nearly as crass as just not asking their permission at all. I can only imagine some dude tweeting me in thirty years to ask my permission to marry my daughter. That would suck ass to the extreme, so I call Lailah and ask her if she wouldn't mind the two of us driving down to Mississippi together so we could do all of this the right way. She agrees, but asks me how I plan to go about it.

"Well, I think it would work if we acted like we'd already been dating for a minute."

"How long do you think?" she asks. "Six months? A year?"

I shrug my shoulders, but then I realize that she can't see me since we're on the phone. "Maybe somewhere between six months and year."

It seems as though we're completely abandoning the idea of just telling our parents the truth, because deep down we both know what we're doing would probably sound ridiculous to anyone who wasn't us.

"So when we go to see your folks, I guess I'll get your father somewhere off by himself and start telling him how I feel about you," I say.

"And I can be talking about us to my mother so she knows how serious we are."

I smile. We're already playing like a team, and that just reinforces how much alike we really are.

"Do you think your father will be cool?" I ask.

"Well, he always thought you were a good person. I don't see why he would start tripping now. You're the son of his best friend, so I'm thinking he probably knew this was a possibility all along."

"And your mother will be cool?"

"Oh yeah," Lailah says. "She has actually told me on several occasions that I needed to just hook up with you anyway. This will be music to her ears."

"Cool," I say, relieved. "Now we just have to tell my parents."

"Do you think they'll trip?" she asks.

"Not at all. I've never made a secret of how much I liked you."

"You told your parents about your feelings for me?"

"It's not like I just bring it up every time we talk, but there have been times when I told them that I'd like to settle down with a woman like you. They agreed that I should make a play for you—and I did —but you know how all of that went down," I say, laughing. "You kept playing a brotha to the side."

"I can't believe that you were telling them about

us the entire time. Now I'm going to feel strange around them."

"Why?"

"I'm the woman who kept turning down their son. That would make me like the enemy or something."

"Seriously? Please. The fact that you're saying yes now will magically undo anything else. I think in the end the result is all I'd care about, so it's probably all that they'd care about, too."

When we get off the phone, I start packing my bag. We'll leave on Saturday morning and should arrive in Daily in roughly five hours. At that point, we'll stop by her parents' house first and then go on to see my parents.

Everything is happening so quickly that I'm still trying to catch up with my thoughts, but I can't help but smile when I realize that I'm finally in a relationship with Lailah.

❦

I DRIVE OVER TO LAILAH'S AFTER I FINISH packing. As I pull into her driveway, a number of things start to dawn on me, and I realize that I have a million questions to ask her. In a way, it seems silly that I'd even have to ask them, but when you haven't been in an intimate relationship with someone, there's a whole side to a person that you just don't know.

That's when it hits me that we should probably be intimate soon. The thought feels almost mechanical when it comes to mind, and I find myself ashamed that I could think of having sex with her as being a requirement for anything, but sadly I can't think of any situation in the modern era where sampling the goods wasn't encouraged.

Standing at the door, I feel the pressure in my guts starting to build, and I hope like hell that intimacy between us comes naturally, because it would suck major ass if it didn't.

"Hey, you," she says, letting me in.

I lean down and kiss her, relishing the feel of her thin, strong arms wrapping themselves around me. I can feel myself coming to attention, so I position myself slightly so that she can better feel that "poke" coming through.

She steps back slowly with a crooked smile on her face. "Well, okay then."

"Boo, you know I can't help it," I offer, singing the lyrics from that song by Next. I know I'm being cheesy, but I can't think of any other response.

"So did you finish packing yet?" she asks.

"Huh?"

"Packing. Did you finish packing for the trip?"

I shake my head trying to understand how we shifted to talking about the trip. "Is everything okay?"

She nods. "Yeah. Why? What's up?"

"It's just," I start, but I can't seem to find the right words to finish.

"Speak your mind, Dizzy, because I can't read it."

I take her hand, and we walk into the den and sit on the couch. I don't even know where to start. In the past few minutes all I could think about was having sex with her—needing to have sex with her—and it's not like we haven't had conversations about sex at least a thousand times over the year (although never about having it with each other), but now I find myself unsure of exactly what to say or how I want to say it. A part of me is even nervous about bringing this issue up with her in such an isolated manner.

Even more, as we sit here, I sense that she already knows what's on my mind but is still insisting that I put the words out there anyway. More than anything I wish that she would be the same old Lailah that I've always known, the kind of person who could read my thoughts and spare me the embarrassment of having to say certain things aloud.

Maybe this is a part of the new relationship we're sharing. If so, I'm going to have to grow a serious pair, because it doesn't seem like she's going to cut me a lot of slack going forward.

"Dizzy, what's up?"

It's only when she speaks that I realize all of my internal debating is causing a room full of silence. By this time I feel embarrassed, so I shift gears.

"How does it feel to be getting married?" I ask.

"Truthfully, I'm still trying to process all of this."

"I feel you." Then I admit, "I wasn't sure you'd even accept my proposal, so I guess I hadn't really thought all that far past our birthday."

"What made you do it? I mean, if you had never brought any of this up, I wouldn't have remembered our agreement—at least not like you did. It might've come to me in six months while I was cleaning the house or something, but it feels like you might have been planning this from the day we talked about it in my dorm room."

I rub the back of her hand softly with my thumb, moving it in slow circles. "I can't believe that we're even here right now," I finally say. "The thought has crossed my mind like a hundred times over the last few years, and now I'm just trying to get used to actually being in this moment after all of this time."

"I don't want our friendship to change, though," she says. "I don't want you to feel like you can't talk to me anymore. Not now. If you start changing on me, that would be my biggest fear coming to life."

"That's your biggest fear?"

"I've been telling you that ever since the first time you told me you liked me. I value our friend-ship that much. You are the one constant denomi-nator in my life, and if you start acting all brand new and switching the script, I think we might need to step back and rethink things."

I shake my head. "I wouldn't change on you, and I definitely wouldn't give you a reason to change your mind. I'm convinced that we can be lovers *and* friends. Aren't you?"

"I'm definitely open to finding out."

I smile, and she leans over and kisses me.

"So are you going to tell me what you were thinking when you got here and why you were acting so funny, or do we have to do some kind of guessing game to get at the truth?" she says.

I know she's right. Even if some of my ideas are crude, silly, or crazy, I can't afford to keep them away from her, especially if they'll affect how we're going to be interacting with each other. "I've been thinking a lot about sex—and about us," I finally say.

I watch as she arches one eyebrow and angles her head toward me. She looks at me with that quizzical expression for a moment before finally asking me, "So what were you thinking?"

IT HADN'T EVEN OCCURRED TO ME THAT WE were both so out of practice with sex that we would be craving the same thing. I thought I was stretching it with my four-month dry spell (a feat that can only be accomplished and sustained with massive amounts of internet porn and lotion), but when she told me that she was approaching a year, I was dumbfounded—in a good way. It was clear that we needed to make up for lost time very soon. The thing was how to do that while still preserving the "integrity" of the situation. The fact that we were having to have an actual conversation about something that two people, in theory, would never really have to have a conversation about ahead of time— not in the mechanical detail that we were—revealed more than a little bit about the awkwardness that has descended upon us.

I don't know if she likes it rough, light, romantic, nasty, or just straight-up gangsta, and I'm afraid to ask, so I just lean in and start kissing her again, slowly moving my kisses to her neck. Her moan is encouraging, so I push on.

"If there's something that you'd like me to do in particular, feel free to let me know," I say.

"Same with you. And if there's something I'm not doing right, don't be afraid to say something."

I reach for her breast, and squeeze it softly through the fabrics of her shirt and bra. Part of me starts dancing on the inside. I have never touched her like this, and just the thought of being here with her like this is starting to give me a full-blown light saber. She clumsily tosses her hand onto my crotch, but she does it so hard that it's like she's smacking my shit with her hand. I wince, but try to play it off. As she starts to stroke me through my jeans, the pain begins to subside.

"That feels nice," I offer, encouraging her.

She kisses my ear lobes, and her warm breath tickles me. I pull away for a second, shrugging my shoulder to my ear. "That tickles."

"You're too cute," she responds playfully. "Where can I kiss you where it won't tickle you then?" Her voice is coy, and for a moment I'm tempted to give her a bullshit answer, but then I remember what she said earlier.

"Are you sure you want me to tell you?"

"I asked, didn't I?"

"Well, I don't think that kissing my balls would tickle."

"Kissing your balls?" she says, looking at me as if my balls were some exotic delicacy from *Fear Factor*.

"I'm sorry. I know that probably came out wrong."

"No, I think you said exactly what you meant. We're in the moment, and you basically tell me you want me to lick your balls."

"Well, you don't have to necessarily lick them. Shit, I didn't mean it like that. I was just trying honesty on for size. My bad."

She takes her hand off of me and sits up straight for a moment. "This is so…*awkward*. Doing it like this. I feel like I'm auditioning for the job of your wife, and that's not the way I want to feel when we make love for the first time."

"I understand. You wouldn't believe how focused I am right now on trying not to mess this up."

For a few minutes we sit side by side not speaking. I begin to wonder if we might be making a mistake by rushing into sex.

"Penny for your thoughts?" I venture.

"I was just thinking that we have everything to lose if this doesn't work."

"You can't think negative."

"It's not me thinking negative. It's me being realistic. What if we're not sexually compatible?"

I take a deep breath before responding, "I tell you what. Why don't we just talk for a while? We've had conversations about sex for most of our lives, yet here we are acting all brand new. We're the ones who're putting all of this unnecessary pressure on ourselves. Let's just talk."

"Okay. I have a question then. What's your favorite position?"

"I don't really have a favorite position. It all depends on the woman, I guess."

"Fair enough."

"What about you?"

"I like to ride, but I don't mind getting it from the back. It depends on how big a guy is. How big are you?"

I could easily just pull down my pants, but I feel put on the spot. "Probably not as big as I was a few seconds ago," I chuckle nervously.

She laughs, and I laugh along with her, trying to relax my nerves.

"I have an idea," I say. "You have a moon window in your bathroom, right?"

"Yeah. What are you thinking?"

"Why don't we just light a few candles, put on some soft music, and take a nice hot bubble bath? We don't have to do anything, if you don't want. I can rub your back and bathe you."

She thinks about this for a moment before rising from the couch. She walks over to her kitchen counter and picks up her iPhone. "Do you still like listening to Me'Shell Ndegeocello?"

"You have some Me'Shell on there? For real? You're truly a woman after my own heart. Please tell me that you have 'Soul Searching' on there."

"Of course. I know how much you love her."

I smile. "Well, I'll go ahead and start the bath then. You get the candles."

&a.

Lailah's tub is large, oval, and deep enough for two people to move around comfortably. Bubbles float above the surface of the water like billowy clouds. She has placed small candles in various corners of the room, and the scent of wild raspberry from both the candles and the bubbles is intoxicating. Just as I remove my shirt, she walks in with her speaker system and places her phone onto the cradle, turning on the music.

I continue to undress, as Lailah fiddles with the volume. I step into the hot water and have to stand still for a moment as my skin adjusts to the temperature.

"Damn, this shit is hot."

"Well, you're the one who ran it, so you can't blame me," she says.

She is now looking at me standing with one foot in the tub, one foot still on the bath rug. I must look like a guy who just got caught breaking into the bathroom, because my body is positioned so awkwardly. I want to smack my head when I realize that this is the first time she's seen me naked, and I have the dumb luck of looking so fucking vulnerable. To add insult to injury, she takes a seat on the lid of the toilet, crosses her legs, and watches me.

"This is fucked up," I say, barely able to budge an inch.

She laughs.

"Aren't you gonna join me?" I ask.

"In a minute," she says. "Right now I just want to look at you."

Once I'm finally able to get both feet into the tub, I begin the slow and arduous process of sitting down into the water. For a fleeting moment, I think of Bugs Bunny sitting down in that big kettle of soon-to-be soup. "Rabbit stew," I mutter.

Lailah bursts out laughing, immediately picking up on my reference. "Why don't you just run some cold water in there to balance it out?"

"That'll end up making some parts of the water too cool," I say, although in reality I'm giving her suggestion some serious thought. Standing there, like my feet are encased in cement, I turn on the cold water. It takes me a minute before I can move my foot and stir it around. I then lower myself into the water and smile. "Yeah, that's perfect."

In my haste to adjust the temperature of the bath, I'm just now noticing Me'Shell singing softly in the background, her heavy voice moving seductively over a syncopated bass and keyboard exchange.

"Join me," I offer.

Lailah continues to look at me without moving. "I just want to look at you for now."

"You already said that."

"I know—but it's true."

"Okay. Don't let the water get cold though. It's perfect right now."

As I sit in the bath, by myself, we talk, reminiscing on what it was like growing up in a place as small as Daily, Mississippi, a place with a population of 15,000, including cats and dogs. We laugh replaying anecdotes of the various things we lived through, but then I remember prom.

"Why didn't we go to prom together?" I ask.

"We really should have gone," she responds. "Teddy Blake was definitely not the move. You know that boy used the whole bottle of Cool Water."

"I could see if he was your boyfriend, but you had to go and pick that bozo out of the blue."

"Well, why didn't you ask me to go then, since you were so concerned about who I went with?"

"After you kicked me to the curb during junior year, I didn't want to run the risk of having you not want me around. I would've asked you if I knew you'd say yes."

She laughs, as she removes her shirt casually. She's not wearing a bra, and even in this dim light, I can tell how amazing she looks. It's been ten years since I saw her like this, and it may as well have been yesterday, because it's like I'm seeing her beauty for the first time.

"Well, that was then. If we could go back in time and you asked, I'd say yes."

She continues undressing and approaches the tub, extending a toned leg into the water. There's a huge part of me that's rejoicing right now, unable to completely process the notion that this woman will soon be my wife. She eases down into the tub, sitting in front of me, her back nestled warmly against my chest. My arms immediately pull her into an embrace, as she lays her head back against my shoulder, her curly hair tickling the side of my face.

"I can't believe that we're finally together," I whisper softly.

She moans, placing her hand on my knee. "It's kind of funny, isn't it?"

As we lie here, I rub her shoulders and occasionally drip hot water from my fingertips onto her chest. Up until recently, I wasn't even convinced that Lailah had feelings for me that went beyond us being friends. It feels as if she must have been considering this for some time, though, and the only thing that was keeping us from being together was this arbitrary line she had drawn. If it were otherwise, she wouldn't be seated in front of me right now. Just being friends who made a deal wouldn't have us taking a bath together—especially with the sexy music of Me'Shell Ndegeocello playing softly in the background.

No. This must be the real thing.

I pull her closer and kiss her neck, my hand working its way toward her inner thigh. She wiggles in such a way that my fingers slide easily inside of her. Her right hand eases around the back of my head and rubs my hair teasingly as she rocks back and forth against my hand.

"I want to look at you," I say.

Lailah leans forward, gripping the tub, and rises, her beautiful figure glistening in the ripple of the candlelight. She slowly turns around, as I scoot forward. Placing her feet on either side of my waist, she begins to lower herself so that she is seated directly in front of me. We begin to kiss as I pull her closer, our moans intermingling with the music as I enter her.

Up until now, I never knew my body could feel this way, and the fact that it's Lailah making it feel this way is all the better.

5

Growing up, I was always afraid of Lailah's father. At six feet four inches, he is a human mountain. Even now, he towers over my five foot ten inch frame. He's the kind of guy who projects a very stern demeanor to everyone around him, but if you get him to laugh, his entire face will light up like a winning slot machine. My father is the quintessential joke teller, so that probably explains why they get along so well. The only reason I know that Mr. Landfair can look stern is because I have seen him when my parents weren't around, and he looks as if he could chew through steel. While it's our plan to go to her parents' house first, I begin to caution the wisdom of asking this man for his daughter's hand in marriage while my parents are not there for backup.

"My father likes you," Lailah says, when I mention all of this to her. We're passing through Tuscaloosa and getting onto Highway 82 West, headed toward Daily.

"How can you be so sure?"

"If he hated you, then you'd know. Trust me."

Her words don't make me feel any better. In fact, it reinforces the idea that her father can be a pretty scary guy.

For a while we drive, just listening to one of the CDs my cousin sent me from his store in New York. I glance over at Lailah as she sings along with a song I've never heard before, but am quickly growing to like. She is beautiful, and the sun coming through the window glows against her skin. I place my hand on her thigh, remembering the feeling of being inside of her.

"I love you," I say.

Her lips peel back, revealing her dimples. "I love you, too."

The feeling of actually telling her that I love her in the romantic sense is still new. But what's even more exciting is hearing her say the words back to me without wondering if she's just being platonic.

I glance at her left hand and realize she's wearing the costume ring I gave her.

"I've gotta get you a better ring. That one was supposed to be a placeholder. I can't have you wearing that around your parents. No telling what they'd think of me for giving you that."

She shrugs. "It doesn't matter to me. I know how expensive rings can be. I just figured you'd give me another ring before the wedding."

That's another thing. In addition to my failing to buy her a real ring, I've been so caught up in the magic of it all (and I'm guessing she has too) that we haven't even set a date. That's one of the things I'm secretly hoping we'll be able to take care of this weekend. But first the ring.

"I think we should pick up a ring before we go to your parent's house," I say, before I realize how crude my words must sound.

"Dizzy, it's not even that serious."

"Your father will hate me, I'm telling you."

"No he won't. And, seriously, if you're going to get me a ring, you should put some thought into what you would like for me to wear for the rest of my life, not just what's available at the mall."

She definitely has a point. "I'm sorry," I say. "I just don't want to give the wrong impression to your folks."

"You're acting like you've never met them before," Lailah says.

"I'm just nervous. That's all."

"If it makes you feel better, I can just not wear the ring at all."

As I see her sliding the ring down her slender finger, I stop her. I remember her hand, years ago, wearing a very similar ring, and it reminds me of just how long I've wanted to be with her. It's as if we've been practicing for this moment ever since we were kids.

"Keep the ring on. If your parents ask, we'll just tell them what I told you when I gave it to you. And I promise what I ultimately get you will make it well worth the wait."

She leans over, kissing my neck. I feel her tongue skating softly along the nape, and I get harder than carbonite Han Solo from *The Empire Strikes Back*.

"La, don't make me pull this car over. You know there are a lot of dirt roads off in here, if you're feeling freaky."

"You're the one who's a freak, Mr. Lick My Balls," she says.

We laugh, as she takes my hand and we ride the remaining distance, mellow in our thoughts, just like the grooves coming through the speakers of my Jeep.

AS SOON AS WE PULL INTO THE LANDFAIRS' driveway, Lailah's mother comes to the front door of their quaint two level country brick house. The house actually seems just as large as it did when we were younger. I remember thinking how much bigger Lailah's house looked than my own, mainly because my house was a one-level wooden house built on an elevated platform (which made it fun to run and jump off of the porch onto the grass below). Even the house Lailah is renting now is vastly larger than my apartment. My guess is that we'll either use her current digs or look for something comparable to start our lives together. I imagine that we'll have that discussion soon enough. The main thing right now is to get her parents' blessing on what we're doing.

"Mom!" Lailah yells, jumping out of the car. Her mother embraces her and rocks her back and forth.

"Come here, Dizzy!" Mrs. Landfair calls out to me, as I walk over and hug her petite, but curvaceous, frame. If daughters are supposed to take after their mothers with age, then I have absolutely nothing to worry about.

"How are you, Mrs. Landfair?"

She whispers in my ear. "You can just call me Mom."

I look at Lailah, and she shrugs at me guiltily. My body immediately tenses.

Still holding me, Mrs. Landfair adds, "I didn't tell Robert. But I'm sure he will be just as excited as I am."

I nod, my smile weakly clinging to my lips. During the entire five hour drive down here, Lailah never thought to mention that she had already told her mother about our engagement, especially after we agreed that we would wait and do that together. Now I feel even more pressure to get this thing right, because now I have two people who will be anxiously watching my performance.

When we walk into house, Mr. Landfair is coming in through the back door wearing a grilling apron that reads "Don't Mess With My Grill."

"Baby girl," he says, scooping Lailah up in his arms and swinging her around like a little girl. Lailah squeezes him tightly, smiling.

"You're grilling? I am so in heaven right now," she says.

"Well, your mother said you and Dizzy were coming today, and I thought it would be good to break out the grill and fire up some chicken and steaks."

Mr. Landfair's grilling is legendary, and I immediately wonder if it was Mrs. Landfair who might have recommended that he grill something, since we were coming to bring some rather gigantic news to the family.

"Dizzy!" Mr. Landfair says, grabbing my hand and pulling me into a massive bear hug. He is so freaking strong that when he grabs me, two drops of bitch come out of me. I'm overwhelmed by his grip, and I feel locked in his smoky smell. The only thing I can think is that this man could crush me in an instant if I ever broke his daughter's heart.

"It's good to see you, Mr. Landfair," I offer, as soon as I am able to refill my lungs with air.

"You guys have a good drive? Didn't pick up any paper from the highway patrol along the way, did you?" he asks, addressing both of us.

"No, Daddy," Lailah says, laughing.

After a few more pleasantries, I offer to assist Mr. Landfair with the grill. He looks at me sternly and points at his apron, his finger touching each of the words silkscreened on his chest: Don't Mess With My Grill. Then he bursts out laughing, his voice booming so that I jump, startled, before the laughter escapes my throat. Both Mrs. Landfair and Lailah laugh along. Truthfully, I know they are laughing at me, though, because they can see I'm an Eddie King, Jr. (or a Heartbeat) short of shitting a brick.

"Come on out here, boy!" Mr. Landfair says, sliding the back door open and stepping out onto the patio.

The grill is massive and looks like the kind of professional equipment Bobby Flay would own. It's clear that the grill is one of his prized possessions. If I were into grilling as seriously as he is, I might very well own an apron that bore a threat to all others, too.

As he walks over by the grill, he checks some fancy knobs, but leaves the lid closed.

"So, Dizzy," he starts, "how is Atlanta treating you?"

"Things are actually going well, sir."

"You still fucking around with those video games? Boy, your parents surprised the hell out of me when they told me you had actually found some people willing to pay you for that."

I swallow. I can't tell if he is insulting me or just poking at me with that humor of his that I haven't been able to completely decipher, even after all of these years. "Things are going well with work. We're making applications for mobile phones these days."

He nods. "I'm going to have to get you to show me how to work this damn phone that my wife got me for my birthday. Damn thing does all kinds of stuff, but I can't seem to do anything but answer it when it rings."

"No problem," I say.

"So how long are you and Lailah going to be in town?"

"Just the weekend."

"Well, it's good to see both of you. Y'all don't come home that much any more, so when you do, I have to break out the grill and make the occasion special."

I nod. "Speaking of special occasions, sir. There's something I need to ask you."

"Sure," Mr. Landfair responds, fiddling with his grill.

I wait for him to stop before I continue. When he realizes that I haven't spoken yet, he stops fiddling with the grill and looks up. "What's on your mind, Dizzy?"

"Sir," I start, but then I hear commotion inside of the house and turn to look through the glass door into the kitchen.

Just as I make out who's inside, Mr. Landfair's voice booms, "They're here!"

When he slides the door open, I'm immediately engulfed in the arms of my mother. She whispers so softly in my ear that I can barely make out each word, but my brain quickly deciphers it anyway: "Have you told Robert yet?"

SINCE MY PARENTS ARRIVED—AND THIS BECAME a get-together for both families—I haven't had an opportunity to talk privately with Mr. Landfair without my father standing right there. As the food finishes grilling, I realize that my best bet might be to just make my intentions known to Mr. Landfair in front of everyone. After all, the four of them are in some way responsible for Lailah and I being friends (and now lovers), and since half of the people in the room seem to already know what's going on, it's up to me to level the playing field for the fathers.

I decide to wait until after dinner, while the six of us are sitting in the dining room preparing to dive into my mom's county-famous sweet potato pie. As people mumble small talk around the table, I rise to my feet and say, "Excuse me, everyone." I immediately see Mom and Mrs. Landfair start smiling, expectantly. The men look up casually. It's clear by the looks on their faces that they have no freaking clue what I am about to say.

I don't know if I should be addressing everyone at the table or just Mr. Landfair at this point. Part of the Southern custom is to ask the father for his daughter's hand in marriage, not the mother. I didn't create that rule, but because of my slight—okay give a brotha credit—fear of pushing the wrong buttons on Mr. Landfair, I was prepared to disregard the implied sexism of such an act and just do things the "old school" way. At least that is what I'd been planning for the past few days. Now, I find it difficult to get around not asking every parent at the table for his or her permission.

"Because of the friendship that all of you have, Lailah and I were born into families with a lot of love to give. And because it was just the two of us as kids, we became close. Lailah has been my best friend my entire life, but if I were to say that I didn't recognize that she was everything I could ever want in a woman, even back when we were in high school, I would be lying. And I can't lie to you all. So I guess it is safe to say that I have loved Lailah all of my life."

I look around the table at each person seated there, and I can't seem to make out what my father and Mr. Landfair are thinking, but they have yet to interrupt my speech with any questions, so I continue.

"Lailah and I have decided that we would very much like to spend our lives together, building on this bond that we've had our entire lives. So I guess what I'm asking each of you," I pause, directing my eyes at Mr. Landfair, "is if we could have your permission to get married."

The mothers explode in celebratory screams, immediately clapping their hands together. The fathers, however, have different looks on their faces. I can't read their thoughts, so I wait for one of them to speak.

My father comes in first. "I didn't even know the two of you were an item." He chuckles as if he could have predicted everything that has happened so far. "Lailah is an amazing woman, and, son, I believe that she will make a wonderful wife. I'd be honored to have her as my daughter-in-law."

My father looks over at Mr. Landfair, as he sits there quietly, his face stern. By now, everyone at the table is looking at him, and my stomach is so full of nervous gas that if I sneezed I'd burn a hole in the back of my pants.

He slowly opens his mouth. "Lailah is my baby girl, my princess. And I knew that when she was born, I would one day have to give her away to some guy. I have to admit I have wondered at times who that man would be and if he would be the kind of man that she deserved, the kind of man who could be strong, yet sensitive and compassionate to her every need. There were even times when I wondered if such a man even existed, since he had not come along. But now I am looking at you, Dominic Parker, a man I have known since you were born into this world, a man who has been like a son to me over these last thirty years, and I am realizing that the man my daughter was meant to be with was right under my nose the entire time."

He pauses to wipe a tear from one of his eyes, and I swear I can't believe I'm hearing these words come from him. My own eyes begin to water, and pretty soon I can hear others at the table sniffling.

"So what I'm trying to say is," Mr. Landfair says, pausing as he composes himself, "welcome to the family!"

He stands up and walks over to hug me. Although I feel my back crack like a bag of knuckles, the love I feel from his hug makes up for the discomfort. In fact, I feel the arms of everyone in the room form into one huge group hug, and for one interminable moment we breathe together as one single family, the way it was always meant to be.

6

———

*S*itting at my cubicle in the downtown space that JACOPLEX has rented, I brainstorm ideas for the next release of our most popular first-person shooter game. At least I'm supposed to be doing that. The entire team has a weekly meeting in another hour, and I want to have a few things to toss out there for their consideration, but I'm still ridiculously excited about the way things went in Daily this past weekend. For a moment while we were at the dining room table, I thought Mr. Landfair (who's requested that I stop addressing him so formally) was going to jump across the table and beat the hell out of me with the jawbone of an ass. I was so relieved when he didn't. And I definitely didn't expect the tears. I think that did it for me right there. If ever I needed a sign that I was on the right track with all of this, then that was it.

I look up at the Storm Trooper clock on the wall above my clump of cubicles. Restless, I walk over to one of the large windows in the old building and look out onto the street. I can see Peachtree Street from here, and it's like a tease.

We're on a side street, just on the edge of Hood Central, but we can see the glamour and glory of the corporate buildings a little more than three blocks away. Our CEO, Brandon Duvall, says that our three-year plan is to move those three blocks to Peachtree. My guess is that we'll scoot up a block each year, or something like that. I'm just afraid I'll have a jheri curl by the time we make it that far.

"Dizzy, my man, what's good?" Akil Dobbs says, as he stands in the entry space of my cubicle. His complexion is almost the same dark brown as the cubicle, and he almost blends in with the walls. I'm actually glad to see him, though. He's probably my closest friend on the JACOPLEX team.

"Chillin'. By the way, I got engaged."

"You *what*?"

"I'm getting married."

"I didn't even know you were hollerin' at anyone. Who are you getting married to? Did you find a mail order bride or something?"

"I'm marrying Lailah."

He bursts out laughing. "Oh man. I thought you were serious. You had me going for a second."

"I *am* marrying Lailah."

"Your friend Lailah? That fine sista who has neva eva eva eva eva given you the time of day?" His mimicking of Chris Tucker's *Friday* lines makes his comment all the more comical.

I realize that what I'm saying to him is probably going to sound ridiculous, given that he actually knows Lailah, so I tell him that we can talk about it over lunch if he pays. He gladly agrees.

Shortly after noon, we walk several blocks to the

deli I hit up at least once a week. After we get our orders, we grab a table next to the back window.

"Okay," Akil starts. "Break it down from the top, because I'm having trouble believing what you're saying. I mean, how in the world did you two go from being best friends to being engaged? I could understand you saying that you guys were messing around. I figure that was going to happen eventually anyway. But this? Marriage? Dude, what the fuck?"

I take a bite of my sandwich and a long swallow of my Coke, knowing that my gestures are only making him more eager. I relish the fact that I have caught Akil off guard. He's such a smart guy, probably the best software and game developer we have, that it's impossible to tell this Negro something that he doesn't already know. Not today though. I have him stumped, and I'm milking this moment for everything it's worth.

Once I have finished my sip and exhaled a patient breath, I start. "Ten years ago Lailah and I made a promise to each other that if we were still single by the time we turned thirty we would get married."

He stares at me for a moment, as if there is a deeper, more complicated explanation on the way, and when I don't say anything else, he shrugs his shoulders. "So you're making good on a promise you made back when you were still young, dumb, and full of cum? Does that even make sense?"

"To us it does."

"She actually accepted? I think that's the part the surprises me most. I know you're the type of person to follow through on something—even if it's just to fuck with someone's mind—but the fact that she went all in with you is the part that's got me fucked up. Did you have to persuade her?"

"Well, kind of."

I tell him the story of how Marcia stepped in and helped to reconnect the frayed wires of my friendship with Lailah and how that subsequent conversation turned the tides. I even tell him about the trip to Mississippi and what it was like asking the families for permission for us to marry.

Akil takes a long swig of his Coke and stares at me, stunned. When he finally opens his mouth to speak, he can only utter, "So I guess you're getting married then. Whoa!"

I nod. "Yeah, man."

"Are you sure you're ready?"

"I'm about as ready as I'll ever be. Why do you ask?"

He laughs to himself.

"What's so funny?" I ask.

"I was just thinking about Jasmine."

"What about her?"

He laughs again. "It wasn't even a year ago that you were all over her like black on Wesley Snipes, and if my memory serves me correctly, you were speculating about a future with her that involved marriage, too."

"It wasn't like that," I say.

"You said, and I quote, 'She is the kind of sista a brotha could settle down with for the long haul.' Yep. You definitely said that shit, because we were playing X-Box at my crib at the time. You kept bringing her up. I was thinking to myself, 'Damn, this nigga is sprung.' Dude, you so were so wide open a Mack truck could have run up through there."

"Well, you already know that she wasn't the one," I say in my defense.

"That's not the point. The point is that you thought that she was marriage material, and now you're saying that Lailah is."

"Hold on," I say. "That's apples and oranges."

"How so? Break it down for me, because a brotha like me only understands shit that is logical."

I take another bite of my sandwich before continuing. "First off, in general, any woman that you decide to actually be in a committed relationship with should be someone you can see yourself being with. Why else would you get in a relationship? If she wasn't someone with the possibility for more, then why not just keep it on the casual tip? So, in my defense, I'll say that any woman I'm in a committed relationship with has the potential to go the distance. But that's it. Just potential. Potential makes the difference between a draft pick and a hall of famer. You know that. Now, on to Lailah. I have known her my entire life. My entire life, man! I have always loved her and longed for her. That's no secret. I just never had a chance until now. Shit didn't work out with Jasmine. She wasn't ready for anything too serious. I get that. But what she did was open up space in my life for real love to come into the picture. Real talk, if Lailah had given up the rhythm, there wouldn't have even been a Jasmine. I know who I want. I've always known who I wanted, and now she wants me. And that's all that matters to me. And that shit doesn't have to be logical, because love ain't logical."

Akil looks at me, his eyes the size of grapefruits. He lifts his hands and starts applauding.

"What?" I say, unclear of what his gesture means.

"You have succeeded, my brotha."

"Succeeded in what?"

"Succeeded in convincing yourself that you're doing the right thing. And for all I know, you probably are. It's just a bit unexpected, that's all. But I'm your boy. I got your back. It's my responsibility to do the gut check, know what I'm saying? I'm not shitting on you."

"For a minute I couldn't tell."

He stands up and daps me with one hand, hugging me with the other arm. "No, seriously. Congratulations, Diz."

"Thanks," I say, as we take our seats again. "We're still planning out the wedding details. When I know what's up, I'll let you know."

"Well, I'll start getting my tux ready. Just let me know where you need me to be and when. And also, let me know when you want to do the bachelor party. I know these sistas who can strip the paint off a Maybach, know what I'm saying? Damn, they get down. These chicks have poles in their living rooms. Do you hear the words that are coming out of my mouth, dude?"

I laugh and breathe a sigh of relief that everyone who needs to know about Lailah and me knows the news. Everyone, except for one person, who I make a point to call as soon as I leave work. I'm sure my cousin, Julian, will probably react the same way as Akil, and the thought of throwing him for a loop gives me something to look forward to for the rest of the work day.

❧

"Yo, J!" I say into my phone.

"Dizzy? What's up, fam?"

"I'm straight chillin' in the cut. Got some news for you!"

"You sound amped like a mothafucka. What's up?"

"My bad, man. How are things on your end? How's Cool?"

"He's straight. The store is doing well. Things are definitely shaping up."

"You'll have to send me another mixtape of those indie grooves," I say. "And put me down for one of the Rare Grooves t-shirts."

"I got you. But I know you didn't call to talk about the store, so spit the shit, dude."

I laugh. I can hear Cool in the background talking to their only employee, Ray-Ray, so I know that J must be sitting out front in the main part of his store. "I'm getting married, man!"

"To who?" he asks, the intonation in his voice reflecting the amplified confusion I figured he would feel.

"Lailah."

"Your homegirl Lailah? I thought she was just your friend. You guys trying to qualify for medical benefits or something?"

"Nah, man. We're in love. Real talk. And we're getting married!"

J is quiet for a moment. "Dude this shit is so far

over my head that I'm gonna have to get a jet pack to follow you. You just woke up one morning and said you were going to get married?"

I walk J through the full story, using a lot of what I shared with Akil earlier in the day. It takes him a moment to grasp everything, but when I'm finished, he says, "I am happy for you, Diz. Seriously. Just let me know when the festivities are. I'll see if I can get Cool to come up for some air and come down to the ATL with me."

"He still with Denise?" I ask.

"Still with Denise? Dude, let me put it to you this way: I expected them to get married before you and Lailah did."

I laugh. "Well, now we have to go to work on you and get you someone."

"I'm doing just fine by myself right now. I don't want to take myself off the market and upset all of these beautiful women in New York City. That would be selfish of me."

We laugh, but deep down I know that J is probably ready to settle down and find someone, but I'm not going to press the issue. I figure he'll do things in his own time.

"Give everybody my best," I say, preparing to hang up.

"No doubt. And I'll get that stuff out to you this week. Be easy, Diz."

7

One thing that parents never tell their sons, especially during those formative years where they are so quick to point out how you should behave around the opposite sex, is how to deal with a woman who is planning a wedding. Nope. They just kind of skip over that part, hoping you will just pick it up on your own, I guess.

Lailah and I have been in discussions all week about this wedding, and the talks have been all over the board. Because of the off-the-cuff way in which we decided to get married, and probably more so because I'm a guy, I didn't think where and how we did it would be all that big of a deal. Boy was I dead wrong!

When the topic of where we would do it came up, in my infinite stupidity, I said—clearly without thinking—that we could just go to the courthouse, because I was more concerned with our marriage than our wedding. The look she gave me could have melted the steel of a Hatori Hanzo Samurai sword. I quickly made a mental note that I would shut the fuck up on matters that might intrude on her fantasies of a full-blown wedding.

After that, we were forced to consider the prospects of getting married outside (a park maybe?), in a civic center of sorts, or whether we would use a church. I knew better than to make any direct suggestions, instead posing light questions that would help her to figure out more directly what she wanted to do. With her Zen practice and the fact that she hadn't attended church in a few years, I wasn't sure she would choose the latter option.

Shows how much I know about my bride-to-be.

She opted for the church, and even more, she wants to do the ceremony in Mississippi, at the church our parents attend, just outside of Daily. I can see the logic in her choice, but even if I didn't, I have adopted this mantra: If she's happy, I'm happy.

I asked her how would planning the wedding from another state work out logistically. She responded that she'd just work closely with our moms to make sure everything came together. I nodded. As long as she was marrying me, we could have gotten married in one of the restrooms at Port Authority in New York City.

Even now as I reflect over the idea of us going back home to get married, I have to smile. Daily was the place where I fell in love with her, so I would never object to going there to start our new life together. I just hope that neither one of us bursts into flames when we walk into St. Peter C.M.E. Church on wedding day due to years of flagrant absences, but maybe we would be okay at a C.M.E. church since we tend to be Christmas, Mother's Day, and Easter kind of folks anyway.

As far as the official date goes, we have given ourselves until next March, roughly seven months. The exact date hinges around the availability of the church and whatever place we use for the reception. If we had our way, though, we would get married during the first two weekends so that we can avoid bumping heads with the legions of college students who will be looking to take their spring breaks.

One thing about being a man about to get married is that you quickly find out that the wedding has nothing to do with how you feel or what you want. The wedding is not for the guy; it's for the woman. She's the one who grew up with the fantasy of a big church wedding, the flowing white dress, the army of bridesmaids, the doves, the flowers, the limousine, and the perfection of it all. She is the star of the show, and I am her supporting cast, just a notch above the other participants. As cliché as this might sound, my job is just to be there and to look my best while I stand next to her.

I don't mind though—mainly because I feel a tug at my heart when I think of Lailah walking down the aisle towards me, her father preparing to give her away. Only in my wildest dreams would I have ever thought such a wish could come true.

The question of how we're going to pay for the wedding is still on the table. Since I gave an old school proposal, I made the assumption that her family would pay for the wedding. I just assumed that was the way it worked. But when I ask her about it, she clams up.

"Well, let me ask you a question. Did your father at least volunteer to pay?"

"I haven't spoken to him about it," she responds.

"I was thinking we should foot the bill ourselves so that we don't inconvenience anyone else."

"I don't think we can get around inconveniencing people when nearly all of the wedding party will have to fly to Mississippi. I'm just saying that we should ask our parents if they would be able to help us out, that's all."

She rolls the idea around in her head for a moment. "I don't want my parents to think that we just pulled this whole idea out of thin air and are coming to them for the money to do it. It would be different if we had been planning this for a while, but after my mother's surgery last year, I would feel kind of funny asking them to come out of their retirement savings to do this."

Well, if her parents are not going to contribute, then I shouldn't put my parents on the line for the whole thing either. That leaves only Lailah and me to pay for everything.

"We would have to do everything on a budget."

"That's what I was guessing."

"And the wedding reception would have to be much smaller," I say.

I can see the furrow between her brows stiffen. I can tell that's not what she wants. She has an idea of the wedding that she wants, and I'm starting to sense that she's going to ask that we pay for it together.

"How much do you have on hand to contribute to a wedding?" she asks.

"I don't really know. I still have to buy the ring and do the arrangements for the honeymoon. I'm going to be serious. I don't think that I would have a lot of flat-out cash on hand. I would have to put things on my credit card, and the limit there is kind of tight."

She sighs and looks away from me. I can't tell if she is angry with me or if she's just considering the situation. I wait patiently.

When she finally speaks, she sounds somber. "We can just do something small, maybe even have a reception in my parents' backyard."

Now I feel guilty, as if I am pissing on a dream that she's probably had her whole life. I want to come up with a magical solution, but I already know that the ring is going to cost me a lot of what's in my savings, and the honeymoon will probably cost me most of the rest. And another part of me considers that if we spend all of our money on wedding re-lated activities, how do we have money to start the actual marriage? Even more, do we want to really start our wedding with debt in behind the events of one day? Maybe it's just the guy in me looking at the situation that way, but I can't help it.

"Can we just talk to our parents and let them know that we're at least open to suggestions on ways of bringing the overall costs down without watering down the actual wedding?" I ask.

"I was hoping we wouldn't have to," she responds.

"I know, baby, but I think our parents would want to help us here, and it would be wrong if we didn't include them in the planning process, espe-cially since the expenses are proving to be more than we could have anticipated. I know my mother would love to not just help with the church. She'll probably insist that she and my father pick up a few things to help facilitate everything. Maybe your parents might feel the same way. We won't know until we ask them."

Lailah shrugs her shoulders, resigned to the fact that we don't really have many options.

"Okay. We can tell them what we're thinking, but let's not make them feel pressured to pay anything. They can help however they see fit. Agreed?"

"Agreed," I say, leaning over and kissing her.

I can already tell that this is going to be a much more complicated process than either of us expected.

❧

"Let me give you three reasons why you need to make me your best man," Akil starts, as he runs his hands along the bill of his Atlanta Falcons baseball cap. We are seated in the food court at Lenox, enjoying an easy Saturday lunch.

"I'm listening."

"I am your closest friend here in Atlanta—next to Lailah."

I nod. "Okay. That's one."

"Truthfully, that's all I should have to say, Negro. But since you want to force it all up out of a brotha, I'll give you the rest."

I laugh and nod.

He picks up where he left off. "I know your girl, so when I help out, I can factor her reaction into the stuff that we will have to do, like tuxes and all that stuff. But the main reason you need to pick me as your best man is because I know how to get the shit poppin' off for your bachelor party! You need someone who is plugged into the know to make that type of thing happen."

I laugh. I know he probably assumes that I am going to pick my cousin J to be my best man, so he is politicking hard. To be honest, J was actually who I had assumed I would ask, him being family and all, but Akil is making some decent points. Even his third point, as funny as it may be, can't be simply ignored. If I'm going to have a bachelor party, it needs to be one that is worth people traveling to Mississippi. Then it hits me. Does Akil realize that the bachelor party will be in a Bible Belt county that has been dry for over three decades?

"I appreciate everything you're saying," I start, "but you do realize that we are going to have to have any type of bachelor party in Mississippi, right?"

"I got that under control, too."

"How so?"

"I'll start making calls to Memphis or Tuscaloosa. There's got to be a major city near Daily."

"Memphis is about two hours away and so is Tuscaloosa."

"See? I know what I'm talking about. I got you, dude. Seriously. Go with your boy on this one," he says, tapping his chest. "I can't steer you wrong."

"Can I think on it?" I finally say.

Akil sighs. "Only if you must. But let a brotha know something soon."

"I got you, but I know you're my boy, thick and thin. And even if, for some reason, I have to go in a different direction with this thing, I know you'll still help send me off in style, so I'm not even tripping on any of this. I just appreciate you putting the perks out there for a brotha to visualize."

He laughs and nods. "I got you." Then he adds, "But you should still pick me."

I laugh, and as we leave the mall, I already know that he is right and that I will.

IN BETWEEN WORKING ON THE STORYLINE FOR the sequel to this fantasy game that JACOPLEX has started developing, I've been contemplating how to deal with the ring situation. I have to shake my head on this one, because, in theory, I should have figured this bit of the equation out long ago, considering that I knew I was going to do this and had had a ten-year head start.

I have two conflicting thoughts on the subject, now that I actually have to do something sooner than later. One is to see if I can find a "real" version of the ring that I have already bought her, using a diamond that I can afford (or afford to charge, given my current financial limitations). If I couldn't do that, I could at least find something that put me in the spirit of the same ring. The only problem with that idea is that I could easily crash and burn by buying her a ring that reminds her of a cheap ring, and the fact that she would be wearing that ring until one of us passes away, I don't know if I could torture her that long with a ring that she really doesn't have much of a liking for. So that leads me to my other option. I could take her with me to a jewelry store and have her pick out a ring that she likes. Maybe I could meet with the jeweler ahead of time and figure out a strategy that could at least guide her to a ring that fit comfortably within my price range.

I definitely would not have been the first person to do such a thing, and if I'm lucky, I will maybe find a jeweler who has had experience doing that particular scenario and who can make the process less stressful.

I decide to wait until I get to the jewelry store before I make my decision.

After asking around, I'm turned on to a jewelry store in Smyrna that is trustworthy, nice, and best of all, affordable. The place is called Steinhem's Jewelry and serves as the place where my CEO, Brandon Duvall (whom we all call Duvall, because that's what he's been called since college) got the wedding ring for his wife. At first I was skeptical, because, after all, he *is* our CEO, but when he told me that he got married way before JACOPLEX and that his budget for an engagement ring was tighter than a gnat's booty, I was more inclined to trust his judgment. After all, I have to buy both an engagement ring and a wedding band to go with it.

The fact that I'm even stressing over this is embarrassing in and of itself. I must have really convinced myself that Lailah would say "no." That's the only way that I can explain my piss poor planning on something as basic as a ring. And to think I thought I was being smooth when I got the costume ring. That costume ring didn't scream engagement at all. Even with Lailah wearing it, although she didn't exactly bring any attention to it, no one thought for a second it was an engagement ring. If so, we would have tipped off the fathers from jump. But we didn't. And unless I get a much classier ring, we won't be projecting our marriage status to anyone beyond ourselves either.

I add the ring to the long list of things I have to

do for things to go smoothly. I'm already looking at vacation packages for St. Lucia and San Juan, Puerto Rico. The prices will be steep, though, and we're almost guaranteed to bump into a crop of vacationing college students who are looking to drink and party their down time away. I might have to be a bit more imaginative if I want to create the perfect honeymoon.

We have decided to Skype our parents this evening so we can conference about the wedding plans. I'm keeping my fingers crossed that they volunteer to pick up some of the financial burden of the wedding. If not, Lailah and I will just have to be creative. And for a novelist and video game story developer, that, in theory, wouldn't be the worst problem to have.

8

We decide to Skype our parents separately, one after the other. Because I know my parents will more than likely be willing to contribute to the wedding funds, I don't want to place any pressure on the Landfairs to do so (although I am secretly hoping like hell that they do). Lailah agrees that we should talk to her parents first, although I haven't revealed to her my rationale, nor have I asked for hers.

As we hover over Lailah's MacBook Air, checking the screen to see if Lailah's parents are connected yet, I have a fleeting thought of just how fast all of this is happening. Not even three weeks ago, I woke up in the morning, *single*, my life just moving along from project to project, and I had a best friend I was semi-secretly crushing on, although I had resolved myself to the fact that was all it would ever be. Then I remembered that night in the dorm room and how close to her I felt, as we sat on her bed. At that moment, I wanted her so badly I ached inside. An ache like that might dull over time but not go away, and something that deeply ingrained in my subconscious was bound to return to the surface, especially with our thirtieth birthday approaching.

"Can you hear me now?" Mrs. Landfair says, poking at the camera on their computer. It's pretty comical seeing how confused she looks, but I would imagine that my own parents would be just as hapless, if I hadn't taught them how to videoconference a year ago.

"We see you, and we hear you, Mom," Lailah says, laughing. "Can you hear us okay?"

Mr. Landfair leans into the frame. "This is amazing! These computers. Boy!"

"Can you hear us?" Lailah repeats playfully.

"Oh yeah, we can hear you, baby girl," Mr. Landfair says.

Mrs. Landfair starts waving at us. "I can see you, and I can hear you. It's just like you're here!"

Once the novelty of what we're doing begins to level off a bit, Lailah begins by telling her parents about our desire to get married at St. Peters C.M.E. Church in Daily. No sooner than Lailah gets it out does Mrs. Landfair dive into suggestions for how to orchestrate both the wedding and the reception.

"Well, Dizzy," Mr. Landfair says, interrupting his wife as she goes on about possible color schemes. "We are the men, so I guess we just let them hash that out. Dot and I will take care of the wedding and reception expenses on this end."

"Daddy, are you sure? Dizzy and I are capable of taking care of all of the expenses. After all, we're the ones who decided to do this, not anyone else."

I bite my tongue. What is she talking about? We need them kicking in or we will go broke with the wedding. I think I know what Lailah is thinking, but in this moment, I am not totally sure. I am just hoping like hell that she is using some type of reverse psychology or something.

Mr. Landfair responds, shaking his head. "We are covering the wedding and the reception, and that's final. I can't let my only daughter pay for her own wedding. What kind of father would I be if I sat back and did nothing to contribute to the happiest day of her life?"

I feel a tug in my chest as I see the way he is beaming at her. In all of my pragmatism I missed some of the emotional components of this. Just seeing Mr. Landfair and Mrs. Landfair on the screen, their smiles so strong that they are beaming love from over three hundred and fifty miles away, I realize just how fortunate Lailah and I are to have them in our corner.

"We truly thank you," I say, unable to conceal my own smile. I can't deny that I'm pleased that we won't go into debt on the wedding, but I'm even happier to know that I'm being welcomed into such a loving family. And that's more than I could have hoped to expect: in-laws who don't treat me like an outlaw.

❧

THE TALK WITH MY PARENTS GOES JUST AS smoothly, and my parents offer to make a contribution to our honeymoon and to help with the food for the reception. By the time Lailah and I close up her MacBook Air for the evening, the only expenses really lingering are her dress, the rings, and my part of the honeymoon. All of a sudden, the budget seems incredibly workable. I feel as if the world has been lifted from my shoulders and I don't have to pretend to be Atlas anymore. I think the thing that makes me the most relaxed is that both of our families are so supportive of what we're doing. It's all going so smoothly that it almost seems like our parents must have been planning this day since we were born.

"So how are you feeling?" I ask Lailah, as we walk back to her den.

"I'm relieved. But I'm still a little tense."

"About the wedding?"

"No. A sista needs to get relaxed, if you catch my drift."

I shrug my shoulders. "I must be missing something."

"Damn, Dizzy! Do you want a sista to come right out and say it?"

"Say what?" I ask, playing along.

She leans in and whispers, "Dizzy, I want you to beat it like a cop. Wee-ooh-wee-ooh-wee! Is that cool with you?"

"Shit, La, that's all you had to say," I respond in my best Sam Jackson imitation from *Pulp Fiction*.

We head back into her bedroom, and this time we don't make love. We fuck like the last two people on the third rock.

And the shit is good!

9

The funny thing about being on a roll where things are going well is that something always creeps up and raises the stakes a bit. In these past few weeks, things have been perfect, so much so that I'm having to pinch myself. I don't know if it's because all of this is still new or if it's because we really want to make this work. But all of that runs through my mind while I'm awake. When I go to sleep, it's a whole other story.

I keep having these dreams about Jasmine, my ex-girlfriend from roughly a year ago. In the dreams we're having ferocious sex all over the place. I keep seeing this large, four level house, and we start in the basement, where I tease her and follow her to the back wall, where a secret set of stairs rise up throughout the back of the house, taking us up level by level, as we sneak through the populated house, looking for a place to unleash ourselves in a fit of ecstasy. In some of the dreams Lailah is there, but I'm sneaking with Jasmine between floors along this hidden path, so she can't see me. Just before I climax in the embrace of Jasmine's mahogany embrace, her calves hiked up by my hips, the sides of her bare feet caressing my legs, I wake up. I have had this dream several times, some times at my house when I'm alone and other times when I'm staying the night with Lailah. Each time when I wake up, I feel guilt shrouding me, as if I've actually done something wrong.

Jasmine was definitely an uninhibited, shit-talking libertine, and being with that kind of woman, especially in a monogamous relationship, can mess a brotha up if he tried to carry that type of thing on to the next woman. Even now I can remember the sound of her voice saying, "I'm going to undress you and make a banana split out of you. You dare me to lick you clean?"

"You had better," I would respond, trying to maintain some sense of authority, although inside I was jumping up and down like a kid who had just won a chance to meet Elmo in person.

With her desire to satiate every single sexual desire that I had, it didn't take me long to drift towards an addiction with her. It was that addiction that urged me to try to guide her toward the altar. When she started pushing away from me, I became scared and tried even harder to hold on to our relationship. In the end, she decided that she needed space, and she started avoiding my phone calls. Not being around her or inside of her was like going cold turkey. After the kind of rigorous sex that we had, I had to take to handling my business far more frequently. I hesitate to think that if my hand was made of sandpaper, I would have whittled myself down to a needle—all while replaying the shit that Jasmine used to do to me, over and over again.

That was a year ago. A year ago. But it feels like it was a lifetime ago. Or it did until I started having these dreams again.

While Lailah and I have done a variety of positions and styles, she hasn't come anywhere close to the kind of freaky shit Jasmine did. In all fairness, though, we have only been together a few weeks. I still wonder how she would react if I started talking shit, breaking out the handcuffs, playing with the toys I keep hidden in a drawer in my room. My favorite is a modified bullet that I use while giving head. I call the lick and vibration exchange "dodging the bullet." Even though I think she would be cool with it, I wouldn't want her to come out of the zone completely by asking me where I got that thing from or who I might have used it on in the past. I'm not sure I even want to open that can of worms.

Then the thought hits me: is it true what they say about married couples having boring, infrequent sex? I hope that was spoken by someone trying to market the notion of staying single, because if there's an ounce of truth to it, I might be up shit creek without a paddle at this point. But as Akil tells me from time to time, don't worry until you have something to worry about.

I decide to keep the dreams a secret, not even sharing them with Akil or my cousin J. What would be the point? I'm getting married, and I love Lailah. And in the end, that's all that should really matter. Right?

❦

THE JEWELER I DEAL WITH AT STEINHEM'S IS A

heavyset white guy with closely cropped gray and black hair. His nametag reads Seth, and he's eager to assist me when I mention that I'm looking for an engagement ring and matching band.

"I would like to see some things that are nice, but affordable," I say, already feeling like a cheapskate. I have to remind myself that I am also paying for a sizable portion of the honeymoon—and then there are the incidentals that come with us moving into the same place and getting furniture and appliances we can agree on. (Truthfully, I'm not picky. As long as I have a man cave, I'm cool.)

"Were you thinking of a cluster or a solitaire?" he asks.

It's a fair enough question, and while I know that a cluster could save me a great deal of money, I have to think down the road. What will I want Lailah to be wearing when she accepts that Nobel Prize for Literature? Maybe a combination of the two? But a solitaire needs to definitely be in there somewhere.

"I'd like to see some solitaires, with maybe some smaller diamonds around it."

Seth begins walking me through the three C's: color, clarity, and carat. I look at a variety of stones with the eyepiece on hand in the store. After about half an hour, I'm pretty convinced that a 1.5-carat princess cut solitaire is what will be the heart of the ring. The price tag is steep, but I can probably get a lift on my credit card limit and pay it off aggressively with my next few paychecks. If I have enough time, I might just save up for it with cash and buy it outright. That would be ideal, if everything came together properly.

Seth shows me a few more rings, which are smaller and less expensive. These will be the rings that Seth and I will show her first, and if things work out well, we will end at the princess cut. I tell him about the costume ring that I bought her, and he agrees to fashion a 14 karat gold version of the ring, using the solitaire in the center and putting much smaller diamonds along the outer edges of the design.

Leaving the jewelry store, I am feeling pretty good about how things are going, and I take out my cell phone to call Lailah when I hear someone calling my name. I turn around, and for a moment it feels as if my heart has just stopped beating.

I swallow and tell myself to man up, to focus and be strong. I refuse to be someone's bitch today.

"Dizzy," Jasmine repeats, pseudo-trotting towards me in her stilettos. Her dress is two inches above the *middle* of her thigh, and her body is even more bodacious than I remember it. She reminds me of Ki Toy Johnson, the video vixen from the Outkast videos. Every part of her is screaming, "I will rock your world!" Even her shirt rises above her navel as she moves, revealing a flat stomach, a navel piercing, and the hint of a six-pack. In the words of my cousin J, she is highly fuckable.

As she leans in to hug me, I can feel her pressing her chest against mine. The smell of her perfume reminds me of the scent she frequently left in my bed sheets. I loved that scent, and when she wasn't there with me, I would take her pillow and hold it in my arms as I slept. It was a poor substitute, but it was a reminder that as long as I could smell her perfume, she was close at hand.

"Look at you. Looking all smooth. You look like a brown skinned DeBarge," she says, inspecting me in my v-neck sweater and jeans.

"Is there such a thing?" I say, laughing. "Look at you! You look like you just stepped off the set up a movie."

"I wish. What are you doing over on this side of town?"

It almost comes across as accusatory, as if in our breaking up, we had somehow subconsciously agreed to adhere to certain geographic boundaries so that we never came in contact again. I'm not sure she intends her comment to be taken that way, so I chill and let it roll off of my back. Still, I want to let her know that even as good as she looks, she can't faze me.

"I'm actually looking at some engagement rings," I say.

Her eyes widen, and she couldn't hide the shock if she were wearing a Halloween mask. I wish I had a camera so I could take a picture of her. That way when she crossed my mind later on in the future, I could look at her face and know that I had successfully transferred all of that negative energy right back on to her ass. The picture would be the proof that I had flipped the fucking script on her.

"You're getting married?"

I nod, not feeling the need to elaborate. This situation reminds me of when Ali and Foreman were fighting "The Rumble in the Jungle" in Zaire and Ali clocked Foreman in the eighth round. Right when Foreman began to turn and fall, Ali had a moment where he could have hit him one more time—just for good measure—but he didn't. He just let

Foreman fall on his own accord. That is how I want to leave Jasmine today, falling off kilter on her own momentum.

"Who in the world are you marrying?" she says, her voice much more forceful than it probably should have been. She catches herself and repeats the question again, this time her voice a bit more controlled.

"My soulmate," I respond. "Hey, look. I have to run some errands, and I'm on a tight schedule. It was good seeing you, though."

"Yeah. Right," she musters. She looks like she doesn't know if she wants to loudmouth me or not. Instead, she turns her head, rolling her eyes. "Whatever."

She might be doing more than that right now, but I wouldn't know. I have already walked away.

❧

BY THE TIME I GET IN MY CAR AND CRANK IT UP, I'm proud of myself for being able to walk away. But it was anything but easy.

Just remembering how sexy she looked makes me have a fleeting thought of sneaking in one last mind-blowing round of butt-ass-nasty-ass sex, the kind that requires video footage and a lot of licking and sucking and fucking and swallowing, a virtual grown man's wet dream. I turn the music on my radio up loud in hopes that it will drown out these thoughts and wither the erection I'm guilty of harboring like an FBI fugitive.

As I get back onto Interstate 85, my phone buzzes with a text message. While I know I shouldn't be checking it while I'm driving, I still take a quick look. The name on the screen says "Jasmine Reed." Beneath her name are the words *"You r a trip!!!"* I want to call her back and ask her what she means, and as I ponder this, I realize that I really shouldn't care at all what she's thinking. Still, I can't resist the urge to indulge in this bit of theater. And it's in moments like these that men make the kinds of decisions they might one day later regret. When I type, *"What do u mean?"* back to her, I know I have just stepped partially off of home plate. The cleats beneath my toes are yearning for the dirt of the base path, and I'm doing all I can to anchor my heel where it's safest.

That's when my phone rings.

I pick it up and answer immediately.

"How did I know you were going to call?" I ask.

"Because I'm a good fiancée," Lailah responds playfully, and I nearly steer out of my lane. I am so thankful that there were no cars in my blind spot, or I might have caused an accident.

"Hey, you," I say, trying to cover for what would have been a major mishap had I said anything more —or different. I quickly make a note to myself: Check to see who is calling first, and don't assume a damn thing.

"I was wondering if you were up for working on the wedding registry this evening. I promise I won't make it too boring for you. I'll even cook for you afterwards."

I smile. I love Lailah's cooking.

"That sounds like a plan. You have any idea of where you want to set up the registries?"

"Macy's, Target, Wal-Mart, Lord and Taylor,

Bloomingdale's, and Pier One," she says. The list is so matter-of-fact that I realize that she must be reading from a sheet of paper.

"All of those places? Why not just three?"

"Options are important, Diz. Some women have twice as many registries. I called myself going about this as simply as I could."

"Would it make you happy to do the ones on your list?" I ask, hoping to appear to be a selfless, good groom.

"It's really about both of us, not just me. So think of this as a project for us to do as a couple, not just you tagging along."

I hold the phone away from my face for a quick moment and sigh, already dreading the thought of patrolling all of those stores with a price gun, tagging things that we probably don't need anyway. Then I remember a line from Chris Rock when he said, "You should look in the mirror and say, ' Fuck you. Fuck your hopes. Fuck your dreams. Fuck your plans. Let's go make this woman happy.'" Even my favorite emcee, Phonte, uses this line on his album *Charity Starts At Home*. I return the phone to my ear and tell her that I look forward to working on the registry later in the evening.

As soon as I get off the phone, I see that I have gotten another text. When I click on Jasmine's message, a picture of her navel, bare, the top of the playboy bunny tattoo that sits nearly two inches lower, fills my screen with the words *"Do you remember when you were mine?"* resting underneath.

I quickly exit off of the interstate and pull over into the closest parking lot. That's when the fear strikes me. It's not the fear of Jasmine or the fear of

Lailah, but the fear of what I might do if I can't get a handle on my thoughts.

I delete the picture from my phone, but not before staring at it long enough to memorize every flawless inch of flesh. I take a long, deep breath. I can do the right thing, I tell myself. But as I say this, I realize that if I have to tell myself that much my mind is not as 100 percent focused as I thought it was.

And that thought is the scariest of them all.

od bless the person who created the registry scanner, a handheld gun-like device that you point at the UPC label to scan an item into the registry database. Such a device would have probably been greatly appreciated during the time my parents got married, as I'm sure my father was dragged from store to store with only a sheet of paper, a raggedy pen, and my mother's desire for nice gifts.

The first place Lailah and I hit up is Macy's at Lenox. It's been a while since I walked through this store, and I'm reminded of how tiring it is to walk through the various floors. The good thing is that, with a wedding registry, we only have to stay in one section of the store, since most of the wedding gifts are in the same section. Because we have decided that I will move in with her after we get married, at least until we find a larger place we could possibly purchase, I'm unaware of what we actually need for the house. After about an hour at Macy's, I realize that we probably need everything in the damn store!

Towels, china, glasses, kitchenware, linen, a blender, a juicer, an iron, and even an advanced toaster are all things that we have zapped onto the list. Unless Lailah is planning on throwing all of her stuff away, along with mine, we're going to have to put a lot of this stuff in storage until we can find a way to use it.

From Macy's, we go to Bloomingdale's, and then on to Wal-Mart. The idea here is to try to cover all of the financial ranges so if a person were inclined to want to get us a gift but not necessarily deal with the expense of traveling to Mississippi, they could just have the store send it to us. Even more, Wal-Mart is probably the only store that is even remotely in the area of Daily, Mississippi, which means that everyone from our hometown who wants to give us a gift can just pick up something while out shopping for cereal and mouthwash.

By the time we get to Target, I have lost all interest in the list. The novelty of using the registry scanner has long since worn off, and I just want to go home, kick up my feet, and see what's on television.

As we scan things for the bathroom, Lailah says, "I want to run something by you."

"What? Any color will do at this point," I respond.

"No. It's not about the registry. It's about something else."

"Okay. What's on your mind, La?"

She hesitates for a second, and in that single moment, I start to feel that maybe she is about to drop some kind of bomb on me. I don't know why, but I sense that whatever she wants to tell me will probably not make me very happy. I brace myself for anything.

"Do you remember Langston?"

Langston? Hughes? I'm trying to figure out what she is talking about.

"Refresh my memory," I finally say.

"My ex-boyfriend. Two years ago. He ended up moving to Chicago."

I don't know who the hell she is talking about, but that's probably my fault. My aim was always to be in her corner on matters of the heart, and it's quite possible that she told me about this guy, but his name never stuck in my head. I nod, unsure of where this is going.

"He has to come to Atlanta for a conference, and he asked me if we could get together for dinner while he was here. I told him that I was involved with someone right now, though."

"*Involved?* You're *engaged.* That's a big difference."

"Either way, I'm not available."

I must admit that her use of such light language to describe us, especially while we're out and about doing a wedding registry, is a bit off-putting, but I try to keep my growing irritation in check. "So is that all, or is there more?"

She pauses for a moment, unsure of how to take my reaction.

"Remember that I am your best friend in this world, so you can tell me the truth," I say.

She pretends to fiddle with the registry scanner, before finally looking up. "I am marrying you. You are the one I want to spend my life with. I know this."

"But?"

"But nothing."

"You want to meet him for dinner? That's it, isn't it?"

"I haven't seen him in a while. That's all. Everything ended kind of awkwardly, and I was thinking that it might be a good idea to bring some closure to the situation, since I have moved on."

I shake my head, unable to no longer hide my frustration. "If you have moved on, you wouldn't need a resolution."

If we were not best friends, I would have unloaded on her in a variety of ways, but I realize that this is exactly what she feared, should we ever get together romantically, that I would not be there for her to confide in on a personal level. I wrestle with it in my gut to react as her fiancé, but I know she expects me to be able to manage the two roles that I play in her life.

"We could all get together for dinner. That way you two could meet each other."

"Why would I need to meet a guy who broke your heart?" I ask, but what I am really thinking is that it would be very uncomfortable sitting at a dinner table with a guy who had had sex with the woman I was going to marry. Even in a hypothetical situation, it sounds absurd. It's almost like taking a poll at the table by asking the question "what do these two guys have in common?" and sitting back waiting for the inevitable answer that they had both been inside of the sole woman at the table.

"I was just letting you know. That's all," she responds.

I can tell I'm losing her right now—not as my wife-to-be, but as my best friend. I am making her feel as though she will have to hide things from me from here going forward, simply because I'm too sensitive to the realities of her life. We're not even married, but I'm starting to show traces of jealousy, which surprises even me. I push to cover it up quickly. "It's just dinner," I finally say. "If you think it will bring closure to the situation, then do it. I trust that you would never do anything to hurt me and that you would respect the proper boundaries."

I can't even believe the shit that's coming out of my mouth, but I feel as though I have no choice.

"I don't know," she responds. "I don't want to disrespect what you and I have with each other."

"I wouldn't take it as disrespect. In fact, I don't even need to be there. Go have your dinner," I say, before adding, "and then come home to me."

She smiles. "Well, if I decide to do it, I will let you know. He is supposed to be coming through next weekend."

I relax my brow and offer simply, "Whatever you decide, I'm cool."

We continue with the registry, and it takes everything that I have inside of me to not dwell on what decision she will ultimately make. I'm no fool. I realize that I might not have been her first choice for a husband, but I know I can't walk around feeling like a number two choice or else our relationship will always suffer for it.

"I love you," she says, as we get into my Jeep.

I look at her smile, broad and glowing beneath the light of the lamps in the parking lot. Something inside of me tells me that I can trust this woman with my life, that she is and has always been my ride-or-die chick. She would never hurt me. Of that I am convinced, so it's not difficult for me to respond to her immediately. "I love you, too."

11

My cousin J doesn't say much to assuage my concerns about Lailah's upcoming dinner with her ex-boyfriend. Not long after we got home, she told me that if I was still cool with the idea, she would meet with him for dinner and that she would make good on hooking me up later. I still don't know how she would be able to make it up to me on a favor so big, but J seems to have some ideas.

"So let me get this right. You gave your fiancée permission to go out with a dude she used to fuck? Okay. I get the fact that you guys have been platonic friends since forever and all, but dude, you must be the craziest Negro in all of creation, trumping the likes of even O.J.! I mean, seriously, however you choose to come out of this will definitely define what kind of man you are."

Now I feel like shit. "What do you mean?" I ask needlessly.

"You said that she would make it up to you, right?"

"Yeah."

"So what did you have in mind?"

"Nothing really," I admit.

I can hear the wheels in J's head turning.

"What about Jasmine?"

"What about her?"

"If Lailah can go out with her ex-boyfriend, then you should be allowed to go out with your ex-girlfriend. That's only fair, when you think about it."

Sadly, up until now, the idea hadn't even crossed my mind, but now I'm having flashbacks to the picture Jasmine texted me several days ago. I imagine her standing in my bedroom, naked, her body so much like a superhero's that I used to call her Storm. And oh could she make it rain!

I tell J about the picture and what the experience of running into her recently was like.

"Sounds like she wants a chance to say goodbye to you, too."

"I think she just wants to prove to me that she still has power over me, regardless of who I'm with."

"And how is it a bad thing to have her believe that? If anything, it just means that you're still on her mind. Trust me. That's a problem that you would want to have."

I shake my head, not sure if I should even be listening to J at this point.

"I don't think going out with Jasmine would be a good idea. She's likely to try to fuck me and blow my mind so that I will have fucked up everything with Lailah."

"You don't trust yourself?" J asks. "You are honestly telling me that you don't trust the love that you have for the woman you have been pining over since you were born? That some sexy woman can control the purest and truest love that you have ever known?

Dude, I think you're seriously underestimating yourself."

I see what he's trying to do. "I trust myself."

"Well, you don't sound like it. Get your balls about yourself, dude, because from where I stand it seems like you trust her with her ex-boyfriend more than you trust yourself with yours."

All I can hear is him saying that I trust her more than I trust myself, and that comment makes me feel like I need to prove such an assumption wrong.

"Now if Jasmine really does have you pussy whipped, I would leave the situation alone, but it's like John Witherspoon said in *Boomerang*, 'Don't be pussy whipped! Whip that pussy! Bang! Bang! Bang!'"

I double over laughing. When I can finally speak, I add, "There's only one pussy I plan on whipping!"

"So it shouldn't be an issue with Jasmine then."

"We'll see."

Long after I get off the phone with my cousin, I'm still pondering his advice. He just has all of these theories about relationships that usually hold a lot of water when tested. I remember when he told me about his B-Sides and Remixes theory, the theory that most people don't reveal their true selves until after the third month of a relationship. I thought he was just saying some shit, but I realize that he was right when he said that the first three months are actually Side A, while everything afterwards is Side B, the part that the public doesn't see and the radio doesn't play, yet it's the side that we live with when we decide to get into committed relationships. Although Lailah and I haven't been engaged for three months yet, I figure that this particular theory doesn't apply, especially since I have known Lailah my entire life.

But would I have guessed that she'd ask me if she could go out with an ex-boyfriend while we were walking around doing our wedding registry? I mean, who does that? On some level such a thing just seems disrespectful. My initial guess is that Lailah clearly doesn't view it the same way, because if she did, then she wouldn't have put me in such an awkward situation at such a bad time. I think she might have been completely oblivious to all of these things.

Is this a glimpse of her B-Side? Maybe. Maybe not.

Either way it goes, I've decided that if she can go out with her ex just to make sure that there is closure to their defunct relationship, she shouldn't be the only one.

&

ALTHOUGH IT SEEMS LIKE A QUESTIONABLE move, I text Jasmine the following day. I send her a very simple message that I know will pull out a definite response.

Sorry about the other day. A lot is going on.

It takes less than three minutes before I receive a response.

Np. ;)

The emoticon makes me pause. Why is she winking at me? I can't lie. The wink is like a tickle to my navel.

I have already decided that I will not press the issue too far, but I do want to soften any antagonism that might still exist from the last time that I saw her.

So when is the wedding?, she texts.

I wonder just how much I need to be saying. The way that many guys get undone is by confiding too much of their business to women who are not their girlfriends. I have heard of the side woman knowing so much about the main woman that she would forever have the guy (and his woman) over a proverbial barrel for as long as she was around, like a hanging blade swinging precariously over his head, able to drop and cut right through him at any moment.

I decide to deflect the question.

Didn't know u cared :)

A few seconds later she responds, *whatever man.*

Then I text, *So are u off the market yet?*

I feel my stomach starting to tense. What exactly am I doing? I feel as though I am walking into a vault with the door locking shut behind me. This might have been cool if all of this happened before I proposed to Lailah, but now the situation is downright spooking me out. I can feel that I am on the verge of playing with fire, and frankly, at this point in my life, I don't know how well I can juggle that.

When I feel my phone vibrate, I see her response: *Nothing serious.*

At this point I have reached the farthest distance that I care to go with this right now. I know that we have an open connection, but just how open is what weighs on the back of my mind. I am almost afraid of what it would be like to be alone with her at this point. I keep seeing her, naked and dancing, when I close my eyes. I see her rotating her hips, one leg elevated on the edge of my bed, while my face rests beneath her vulva. I can still taste her, as I stroke my hand up and down her lifted calf.

I shake my head and immediately force a memory of Lailah to the front of my mind. I think about how long it took me to get to this point with her. Every kiss, every caress, every embrace. I waited a long time for those things. And now that I have hit the jackpot, I am looking back at a scratch card from the neighborhood corner store. What the hell is wrong with me? I can't possibly be this weak. I refuse to believe that.

I put my phone down. I am done with texting today. I found out as much as I care to find out, so I'm tabling everything for now. I am now beginning to question whether I can go through with this. But then I remember that Lailah has no problem going out to dinner with a guy she used to fuck, a guy that, in theory, might still hold some sway over her. After all, that is the point of doing something to bring closure. It is a subtle admission that there is something about that person that still has a hook in you after all of this time, and by meeting up one last time, you are hoping that you can unhook yourself from that individual (with his or her help) permanently. I can't help but wonder why a person would get engaged if he or she still had hooks in them. But then I am a prime example of someone who is still pining over his past.

Maybe I need to meet up with Jasmine more than Lailah needs to meet up with her ex-boyfriend. I can't help but think that if she thinks meeting up with him will help our relationship to survive the long haul, then I need to find a way to permanently put Jasmine in my rearview mirror.

That doesn't make the nervousness subside though. In fact, the only thing I can do now is tell myself to man up, to grow a pair. If I am doing this for the right reasons, then there is nothing wrong with seeing Jasmine again. Plus, I would hate to be out and about somewhere with Lailah and feel as though Jasmine still holds some kind of sway over me. That would be a horrible look for Lailah and me, and her knowing that there was a woman out there who could derail our marriage whenever she saw fit would stress the hell out of our relationship. Lailah doesn't deserve that, and I would never wish her that kind of pain or frustration.

I just hope that Lailah feels the same as I do.

12

At the beginning of our junior year of high school, I knew what I had to do. After a torturing summer of seeing Lailah become sexier and sexier, I was more convinced than ever that I needed to play my hand. I had been holding my cards to my chest for years, even back before she had breasts. Now she was the full package. There was no one at Daily High who could touch her with a ten-foot pole. She had it going on with her naturally curly hair pulled back into a bun. Junior year would be the year that I would make my move, but I found that I would clam up every time I was around her. So not only was I not advancing my agenda, but I was also making our existing friendship incredibly awkward.

Then I got the idea to write her a letter where I told her how I really felt about her and what I felt that we could have together, if we gave love a chance. I composed at least ten different versions of the letter, laboring over every word, before deciding to throw them all away and try something different.

After the failed attempt at the letter, I thought I

might be able to compose a song on the piano for her, Brian McKnight style, and do my best to sing my feelings to her. Every day while my parents were at work, I would practice the song aloud, sometimes recording myself so that I could hear how I sounded. (I can carry a tune, but that's about it.) I could never get the song to sound the way I wanted it to sound, and I either went too strong with the lyrics or too soft with them. Either way, I wanted Lailah to take my feelings seriously and not get wrapped up in the non-singing version of my love song to her.

Interestingly, the idea for the song led to the classic cliché of all time, which I am not ashamed to admit that I indulged: putting together a mixtape of songs about budding relationships. I had everything on the CD I made for her, from Mint Condition to Brian McKnight. The CD had oldies and stuff that was out and hot at the time. I had even arranged the songs so that they progressively told the story of our time as friends and where I hoped that we would go as boyfriend and girlfriend. The first song, I thought, said it all: "I Remember You" by Brian McKnight. I figured that if she heard that one first, she would know where I was coming from and hopefully follow me the rest of the way through the CD.

When I gave her the CD, she listened to it, and said that it was cool. And that was it. Nothing more. It took me a week before I realized that she just didn't know what I was hoping to accomplish with the mixtape. She apparently had thought that I was just giving her a tape of songs that I thought she would like. That left me little choice but to just break down and tell her what was on my mind.

By this time, it was November and the air outside was crisp and cool, the leaves already having fallen from the trees. We were standing out in the parking lot of the school, cloaked in bubble down goose feathered jackets and toboggans, and I can distinctly remember how beautiful her face glowed as she looked up at me. I struggled with my words for a minute, but she was patient with me, something that I had always appreciated about her friendship.

When I finally formed the words with my lips, I said, "There is something that's been on my mind for a while, and I have been wracking my brain trying to figure out the best way to say it."

"Oh, Dizzy," she said, her voice turning downward, as she began to shake her head. "Don't do it."

"Do what?"

"Don't say it."

"How do you know what I'm going to say?"

"Because I know you."

For a moment I didn't know what to do. I had been rehearsing what I would say to her for so long that I didn't know how to put the breaks on my feelings.

"I just have to tell you something."

"Dizzy, you're not listening to me. You do not have to say anything."

Somehow I had convinced myself that she couldn't read my mind, that she had just missed the point when it came to the mixtape, that it was my responsibility to step up and be bold and tell her exactly how I felt, so I did.

As I stood there telling her how I felt that we would be good together and how much I cared about her, I don't know what I thought she would say in response, but in my dreams I had hoped that she would fall into my embrace and hold me with the tenderness that I so desperately craved.

"Dizzy, you're my best friend. Best *friend*," she emphasized. "If we start dating and it doesn't work out, then where will that leave us? I want to always have you in my life, and the only way to guarantee that is not to complicate things."

I was so shocked and hurt at the same time that my mouth stopped working for a second. When I finally got it to work, I said, "We are just taking our friendship to a new level. That's all. We won't stop being friends just because we open this new door and walk through it."

She shook her head slowly, as if I wasn't getting the bigger picture. "I love you, and I want to always have you in my life. I value you more than having you as just my boyfriend."

I could feel the sting, but there was a salve in her words. We went on being friends all throughout high school, even taking different people to our senior prom. It was clear from the look of things that being friends was all we would ever be to each other.

What she didn't know is that I was prepared to wait her out. Clearly, I was in it for the long haul.

Even now that we are thirty, there's a kind of Irkle-esque quality to our relationship. Apparently, I wore her down, but in each kiss that she gives me and each time she wraps her body around mine, I don't sense any regret in her decision.

❧

WE AGREE ON FIVE GROOMSMEN, INCLUDING the best man, and five bridesmaids, including the maid or honor. That part does not take all that long. I already know that Akil and J will be topping that list anyway. Where things get a bit more interesting is when Lailah breaks out several swatches of fabric combinations.

"These are some of the colors I was thinking we should use for the wedding," she says.

I immediately kick into groom mode. "Whatever you think is the best combination is the one we should use." Only this time my deference doesn't work.

"Dizzy, seriously? Are you going to do this for the entire planning stage?"

"What do you mean? I trust your judgment."

"You just don't want to have anything to do with this, do you?"

"That's not it at all. I am here with you right now because I want to be. I just figure that your taste in things is so much better than my own that I didn't want to drag us down with my unnecessary input."

"You are the man I am marrying," she says. "Would it be too much for us to make some decisions together?"

"We are. I am voting on whatever you decide."

"Damn, Dizzy!" she says, exasperated. She stands up and walks out of the room, leaving me in her den with the swatches laid out on the floor. I am still trying to register what just happened. Is she really mad at me? Over some swatches? I shake my head and try to get a handle on things as I stand up and start to walk toward the kitchen, where I see her leaning against the counter drinking a glass of water.

I don't know what to say, so I just start apologizing, since I figure that would cover everything that I must have done wrong in the last few moments.

"You don't get it at all. Do you?" she answers. "I bet you don't even know what you are apologizing for."

"Truthfully? No, I don't, but I hate the fact that I set you off, and I want to make it right."

She laughs sarcastically under her breath. "If you want to make it up to me, go in there and pick out the swatch combination that you like and bring it to me."

I turn around and head back into the den. I glance at the pinned colored squares on the floor. There are four combinations. One is a light tan and a cranberry red, another is navy blue and silver, and the other two are baby blue and cream and a reddish pink pinned to an almost white silver. They all look nice, but I have convinced myself that this is something that she should be doing with Marcia, not me. But why do I feel that way? Has she ever really given me any reason to not feel like I could contribute to the decisions involving our wedding? Not that I can think of.

I also think about when we were doing our registries and how I had deferred to her. She seemed like she was cool with that, so I thought I might have mastered the first rule of married life: staying out of my wife's way on matters that are largely subjective to her personal tastes. Plus, we will be living in her house, so I figure she has a better idea of what colors would work on the registry items and what appliances she would want to have. I thought that just loving her and pledging my undying love to her was my job and that the superficial particulars were things that she could decide, and I would step in only if I needed to.

Now I am starting to suspect that she wants me to be an equal partner in planning the details of the wedding, so I grab each of the swatches off the floor and walk back into the kitchen.

"I told you to just bring in the one that you liked," Lailah starts.

"I like all of them."

"So you're not even going to try to help me at all?"

"Actually, I am," I say. "I figured I would tell you what I liked about each of the combinations, and hopefully we can discuss what you liked about each of them, since you selected these few."

She nods, unsure of whether she should yield on the hostility. I move quickly before she fires up the venom again.

"I think that each of the combinations is nice, but I noticed that the baby blue and cream and the pink and silver are the softest colors. While I love the navy blue, it seems a little heavy a color to use in March. And if the temperature continues in the same cycle from last year, it will probably still be a little cool in March. That's why I am leaning toward the cranberry-ish color with the light tan color. It's not heavy or light. It seems like it could be a nice complement to that time of year."

Lailah listens, nodding as I finish my argument. Up until I opened my mouth, I really didn't know which one I had a preference for.

"Cranberry and champagne," she says.

"What do you mean?"

"The color is champagne, not tan." She chuckles

and walks over to me, wrapping her arms around me.

"So did I do okay?"

"Yes, you did. I was going back and forth between the rose and silver and the cranberry and champagne anyway."

"So we are going with the cranberry and champagne then?"

She smiles. "Why not?"

I kiss her tenderly, relieved that I managed to come through this experience unscathed—at least for now.

"You would have had me wearing a pink tuxedo?" I ask, joking.

"It's rose, not pink. And you should have a white vest to match my gown. The groomsmen would be the ones wearing the rose tuxedo vests to match the bridesmaids dresses."

"J would have killed me!" I say, laughing.

"J would have just had to bite his tongue and wear the colors. I can't see him bailing out on something as simple as the colors."

"You apparently don't know J all that well."

"Well, hopefully he won't have a problem with cranberry and champagne then," she says.

"Who cares what he thinks anyway? As long as the tuxes are nice, he won't even be able to complain."

We walk back into the den and sit on the couch.

"There's something I want to show you," Lailah says, as she leaves the room.

A few minutes later, she returns with a CD and puts it in the small boom box that she refuses to throw away, despite the fact that she has more music on her iPhone than I do on mine. As soon as she presses play, I hear Brian McKnight's "I Remember You." It's the CD that I gave her back when we were juniors. I can't believe that she still has it, that she would have held on to it for as long as she has.

"Man, is that a blast from the past!" I say. "You know, when I gave you that CD that was me trying to make a play for you. I was convinced that each song would tell you everything I couldn't bring myself to say."

"I know."

"You knew? Why didn't you say something then?"

"Back then, I wasn't trying to be with you like that. Don't you remember me telling you that I didn't want you to say anything while we were standing in the parking lot."

I shake my head. "Here I am thinking that you just didn't get what I was trying to say. I figured maybe I was being to abstract with my intentions. I mean, I was totally convinced that you had no idea that I liked you."

"Dizzy, how long have I known you?"

"Forever."

"Of course I knew what you were trying to do. How could I not?" She nods to the music as she listens. "It's all about a boy and a girl sharing that special bond, even as kids. That's us."

I smile. "Yeah. I just wish I knew that then. I straight played myself in the parking lot then."

"No you didn't. You just pushed the point a little past the point that you had to. No harm, no foul, though. After all, you did eventually get me in the end."

Now I'm cheesing. "Yes, I did."

"Want to hear something funny? I was sitting up here after you had proposed, talking with Marcia and she was combing through my Dizzy box..."

"Dizzy box? What's that?"

"That's the box that I put all of the things you have ever given me."

"You kept all of those things?"

"Yeah."

"Why?"

"Because you gave them to me, and you are my best friend in the world."

I start blushing, unable to stop smiling. "So you were feeling me then?"

She mockingly rolls her eyes at me. "Anyway. Marcia was over here and she found the CD in the box, so she took it out and put it in the CD player. I hadn't heard it in years, but it started to bring back memories. That's when I realized that you have always been there for me. You have always been my sounding board. You have always been my standard for the guys I would date."

"Seriously?"

"Yeah. I wanted them to be smart, nice, thoughtful, talented, and handsome. In some way they had to at least have those basic qualities, and now that I think about it, I was really just looking for a man who was just like you—but wasn't you."

"Well, you could have had me anytime you got ready. You were always the one who could have pulled me away from any relationship I was in. But I'm glad you waited, because I am a better man than I was back then. I would have hated to lose you in behind some of the immature bullshit I must have put some other women through."

"So this is what you want? You have to be sure, Dizzy."

"I am more than sure. This is what I have always wanted. This is probably the only thing that I have ever been sure about in my entire life."

"I hope you feel the same way after you start getting pet peeves about me."

"Trust me. I will love you through those."

She laughs. "You sound like you've already found some pet peeves."

"We all have them. It's no big deal."

She snuggles up next to me, and I place my arm around her petite body. "What are some things that you don't like about me?"

"There's nothing that I don't like."

"You just suggested that you have some pet peeves about me."

"I don't dislike them. They are a part of the whole you."

"Come on, Dizzy! Tell me!"

"Why don't you tell me something first," I offer.

"Okay. Sometimes you forget to put the toilet seat down. And sometimes you will leave dishes out rather than just put them in the sink."

"Fair enough. I can work on those things."

"Your turn," Lailah says.

I hesitate for a moment, knowing that the things that I am thinking about saying are things that she probably can't help. I consider just making up something, but when she nudges me again, I tell her, "Sometimes you poot in your sleep."

"No, I don't!" she squeals, covering her face with her hands. "I do not poot."

"Okay, then. Maybe I'm mistaken."

She pushes me again. "I do not poot in my sleep."

"Whatever you want to believe is fine with me. At least I didn't say you farted in your sleep."

"Pooting and farting are the same thing," she says.

"When you're cute, it's pooting, but when you're not cute, it's just straight farting."

She looks up at me, trying to keep a straight face. "Does it stink?"

"Just a little. Smells like sour milk. You're just a tad bit *ruin't*, but not all the way."

She starts laughing and covering up her face again. "I am so freaking embarrassed! I want to just crawl up and die right now."

"It's okay," I say. "If you would like for me to let one loose, I can work up something in a few minutes. That way you won't feel so bad."

She shakes her head vigorously. "No. That's quite all right."

"I'm just saying. Because I can crack a motherfucker off so hard that my ass will be sore afterwards."

"Damn, Dizzy!"

"I let loose. I'm a grown man. That's what I do. It's all about volume and velocity. Shit, I remember one time I farted so hard I thought I had bruised my anus. For real."

"T.M.I.," Lailah says, doubled over laughing. "Too much information!"

"I just don't want you to think that you need to

be embarrassed about doing something that is natural. Just do me a favor and point your ass away from me when you feel it coming on. I swear I thought an ant was crawling up my leg the other night."

She continues laughing, before adding, "I might just give you a Dutch oven!"

"What the hell is a Dutch oven?"

"It's where you pull the covers over someone's head after you pass gas."

"Oh, hell no!" I say, unable to keep a straight face. "Have the whole bed smelling like you pooted corn flakes and peaches."

"Corn flakes and peaches? I thought you said sour milk."

"It smells like all of that."

She playfully hits me on my arm. "You still love me."

"More than anything else in the world."

"Chris Rock said you have to love the crust of a person," Lailah says. "Do you love my crust?"

After I finish laughing, I lean in and kiss her lips softly. "Yes. I love you and your crust."

"Well, I love your crust, too."

13
___

As soon as I make it to my cubicle at JACOPLEX, Gerald Lewis comes around to each of our cubicles telling us that we need to meet up in the conference room in the next few minutes. I look over at Akil, and he shrugs his shoulders.

We head in and grab one of the few remaining seats at the conference table. At the head of the table is Duvall, and seated next to him is a woman in a suit. I have never seen her, but she clearly exudes power. Even Duvall is wearing his best suit today. The rest of us, however, are dressed all over the spectrum from khakis and casual shoes to cargo shorts and sandals. We make games, after all. We don't deal directly with end users.

"I wanted to call everyone together this morning to make a special announcement," Duvall starts.

I can see Akil nibbling on his lip. He is clearly nervous about what is going on, and I can't blame him. I am just praying like hell that we are not getting fired today. I don't know if I would be able to handle that, not with the wedding coming up. I am already feeling guilty about the fact that I am having to move in with Lailah after we get married. I feel like a scrub. If I lose my job, I will be the biggest scrub ever, and while I know she would have my back, I am not prepared to put my marriage to the test so early in the game.

Duvall continues. "I want to introduce you to Mrs. Joanne Bishop. She is the COO of Gameland Media. I'm sure that you are all familiar with the work that they have done in gaming."

I glance at Akil. So this is it. This is how it's all going to go down. This is the part of my life story where the conflict that leads to the climax occurs. I tell myself that being unemployed is not so bad. I will bounce back. I have a degree from Ellison-Wright and over five years of working with video games. I am marketable, I tell myself. I'll survive. Right.

"We have always been a small company, and we have always known that there was only so far we would be able to get ourselves on our own steam. Our staff is small, and I think we have accomplished a miracle, but I also believe that JACOPLEX can be so much more than it is. It's funny standing here like this, but I must confess that I have steered this ship as far as I can, and I honestly feel that another company will need to steer us the rest of the way."

People look around at each other confused, so Duvall quickly adds, "Gameland will be acquiring us. Now, before you go and get upset, let me explain some things. Each of you were issued anywhere from 15,000 to 30,000 in stock when we incorporated. Gameland has agreed to pay $17.50 per share, and I have been guaranteed that the JACOPLEX team will remain actively involved over the next six months with the transitioning of our games to Gameland. After that, Gameland will assume control of everything."

"So we are basically being fired?" someone asks.

Duvall responds, "No one says that you will be fired."

"But you just said six months! After that, it will be up to them to keep us."

Mrs. Bishop quickly stands to speak. "Gameland values what each of you has contributed to JACOPLEX, and in acquiring JACOPLEX, we are just as concerned with the talent that is here as we are with the games that you have created."

"Oh shit!" Akil yells out, surprising everyone at the table.

The room becomes so silent that you could easily hear a mouse pissing on cotton.

"The person with the fewest shares of stock options at this table stands to make $262,500 in cash!"

I watch him continue punching numbers into the calculator on his phone. He looks up and pushes his phone across the table to me, as everyone around us begins to do the math as to how much money they stand to make from this acquisition. I am one of the fortunate ones who had 30,000 shares. I look down at Akil's calculator and my eyes nearly pop out of my head. $525,000! Over half a million? Hell, for that kind of money, I am sure I can land on my feet at the end of the day, whether Gameland keeps me or not.

Duvall tries to seek control of the meeting, but all of us sitting around the table are still trying to figure out how to spend the six figures that each of us will collect. Once we finally settle down, Duvall says, "I guess I should have started with the money part first then."

Akil laughs loudly. "Hell yeah!"

Duvall smiles and nods. He turns over the meeting to Mrs. Bishop, and while we listen to the goals that she has for JACOPLEX as the newest member of the Gameland Media family, our heads are still in the clouds, and the only thing I can think of doing is buying a bottle of bubbly and surprising Lailah with the news.

Duvall gives all of us the rest of the day off after Mrs. Bishop leaves. His net worth just blew north of seven figures, so I suspect he is about to go and do something outrageous with his wife to commemorate the occasion. I am just so glad that I was fortunate enough to ride this situation out. My annual salary was hardly impressive, but a windfall like this makes it worth all of the headaches and the move from New York to Atlanta.

And all of this couldn't have come at a better time. I don't think that I have ever been this high off the ground before, and all I want to do is go home so I can shout my brains out without scaring the hell of those standing around me. Even Akil is not trying to linger. I have no idea of where he's headed, but he ducked out so quickly that I am guessing I will have an anecdote coming from him the next time we meet up.

When I arrive at Lailah's house, she comes to the door dressed in a beautiful and stunning black dress. She is so fine that I have to do a double take. From her small purse to her heels, she looks as if she is about to go hit the red carpet at an awards show.

"Where are you headed?" I ask, holding on

tightly to my good news like a child afraid of losing a helium balloon to the wind outdoors.

"This is the night I am supposed to meet up with Langston. Remember?"

Hell no, I don't remember, but I play it cool. I'm supposed to be happy about all of this, right?

"It must have slipped my mind."

"I'll only be gone a few hours, but when I get back, I'm going to rub your feet and grant you any one wish."

I nod, still unable to believe that she's going to go through with this. I feel like such a fucking fool. Even as I look at her, I realize I haven't even seen her in this outfit before. I hope to high hell that she didn't go out shopping for something to wear just for this dude. My insides are starting to boil over with jealousy, and I'm afraid that I'm going to get seriously ethnic up in this piece and say something I can't take back.

"Have a good time," is all that I can muster.

I walk her outside and give her a kiss on the cheek before hopping in my Jeep and pulling out of the driveway. I am not even down the street good before I have picked up my phone and started searching for Jasmine's number.

&

As I pull up Jasmine's number, I realize that I am still too heated to place the phone call. I drive straight home and sit alone in the darkness of my increasingly cramped apartment. I try to temper all of the anger and frustration I am feeling with all of the wonderful moments that Lailah and I have recently shared. A few times I am able to calm myself down and remind myself that this closure that she is so desperately seeking is a good thing for the survival of our marriage, and then just as quickly as I had managed to calm myself down, I think to myself, fuck that shit! No dude should have to put up with this. What kind of sucker do I have to be to let some other dude take my girl out on a date? Seriously. I must be out of my fucking mind. Part of me even considers trying to find the restaurant they are meeting at—if they are even meeting at a restaurant. I never asked her where they were going. They could very well be meeting up at his hotel to get one last fuck in.

Now I'm steamed. It takes everything in my body to keep from screaming aloud in the room. I am too dignified a brotha to trip out like this, I tell myself. I just got news of the biggest paycheck of my life, and I am only thirty years old. I don't have to sit around taking this kind of shit off of anyone, especially the woman I am supposed to marry, the woman who has been my best friend in the world since the beginning. Hell, I still have enough swagger to pull someone. If I really wanted to, I could probably call Jasmine and she would come over here and hook a brotha up and make him feel like a million bucks—or at least half a million bucks.

I go to my bedroom and lie down on my bed. The darkness of the room feels like the room is closing in on me. I'm having a thousand thoughts a second, and I can't seem to steel my mind. Maybe I should hold off on telling Lailah about the money. At this point, I'm not sure she deserves to even get the news for a while. Then I realize that she is the only person I would have wanted to celebrate this information with. That must be what she was referring to before about not wanting something to happen that would fuck up our ability to be best friends.

I can't stop thinking about the fact that I actually consented to her going out with him. Langston, whatever the fuck his last name is. Who the hell does he think he is that he can just come in out of the fucking blue and scoop up my girl for the evening. No respect at all for me. I should have agreed to go out with them to the dinner. Naw. Fuck that. I'm not trying to be a third wheel in a dick-a-thon.

After I finish being mad at her and then him, I get mad at myself for a good hour, before finding my way back to her. The reason I am so angry and hurt is because she looked so good when I saw her last. She was perfect, amazing, capable of taking my breath completely away and leaving me to die of suffocation. I am not even saying that if she had looked "to'e up from the flo' up" that I would feel any less hurt.

Once I have taken all that I can take of this feeling, I grab my phone and call Jasmine. She doesn't answer, but I leave a brief message for her to call me when she gets a free minute.

I head to the kitchen and pop open the champagne I had bought for the special occasion and take it straight to the head. I polish off the bottle and lie down on my bed. The room swirls around me, and within minutes, I pass out.

When I wake up, I look at my watch. It's nearly eleven. I pick up my phone from the night stand and immediately check for missed calls and text messages. There is one voicemail on the phone. No text messages. I stand there holding the phone to my face, desperately wanting to hurl the phone through my window. Although my head is not completely clear, the anger boils back up. The only message is from Jasmine. Lailah has not called.

She left the house shortly before five o'clock, and nearly six hours have passed without so much as a phone call or text. "What the fuck?" I scream.

The anger before returns with a vengeance. I don't know whether I should be worried that something has happened to her on the road or worried about what she is doing with that Langston guy. I grab the phone and call her number. And then I wait. And wait. The phone continues ringing and eventually goes to voicemail.

I lift the empty bottle and realize that I will not be driving anywhere tonight. No, I will be sitting in my room worried about Lailah, hoping she is okay and that she is still my fiancée after tonight.

To calm myself down, I listen to Jasmine's voicemail.

"Hey stranger," she says. "I'm surprised to hear from you! I am just returning your call. I hope all is well on your end. You can give me a call back whenever. It doesn't matter what time. I'll be up for a while tonight anyway. Talk to you soon."

I turn on the television and watch some show on the Spike channel. It is mindless entertainment, which is exactly what I need right now. I am not yet distracted when my phone rings. It's now 11:15 p.m., and I immediately see that it's Lailah.

I stare at the phone for a moment, weighing whether or not I should even bother to answer it. It's been over six hours and fifteen minutes since I last saw her! She doesn't even deserve my time right now, but I'm desperate to know why she hasn't called. In the back of my mind, I can't think of a single excuse or explanation for why she would have gone incognegro for so long. I am still groggy and there is a dizzying pulse at the front of my head, but I still answer the phone.

"I am so sorry," she starts. "I didn't know it was this late."

At that moment, I just go completely numb. I realize that I just can't afford to care anymore.

"Dizzy?" she asks. "Dizzy, are you still there?"

"Yeah," I respond, my voice flat and listless.

"I really have no excuse, but my phone got misplaced and we ended up having to wait two hours to get a table at the restaurant, and then we were talking for a while."

"Okay."

"Okay, what?"

"I'm just listening. I figure after waiting over six hours to hear from you, I can wait to hear you explain yourself."

"I just did."

"Okay."

"Dizzy, what's going on?"

"You tell me. You're the one who hooked up with your ex-boyfriend for six hours. What the hell am I supposed to think?"

"We just had dinner. Nothing else."

"Okay."

"Let me let you go then. I'm trying to have a conversation with you and you are just being all humdrum and detached."

"Don't put this on me. This is all you."

"I told you I was sorry."

"Whatever."

"Maybe we should just talk later then."

"Peace," I say and hang up the phone.

At this point she can go and leap her fucking ass into a lake for all I care.

I roll the cell phone around in my hand for a moment, wondering if I should call her back and tell her what I have been thinking about for the past few hours. Then I consider calling Jasmine. But there is a part of me that doesn't want to stoop to her level, although I know I am already dwelling there.

I reason that if I'm going to go out with Jasmine, I should do it the same way Lailah did me with Langston, just to see if she will play the double standard card against me. I want to see how she would feel if I were to go out for six hours with my ex-girlfriend and not pick up my phone to call or text. I want her to see what it feels like to wonder about what someone is doing. I also want her to worry about me the same way that I was worrying about her, not knowing if she was in a ditch somewhere or in a hotel in Buckhead. I want her to feel all of the pain I've been carrying around during this fourth of a whole damn day.

There is a part of me that knows that my doing this will not help the situation, but I don't really care at this point. I just want there to be some balance to things. If I have to play the fool once, then she should have to play the fool once.

I know that she will never tell me everything that happened when she went out with Langston, and I don't plan to tell her what happens when I go out with Jasmine. I am guessing we will just keep those secrets from each other like other secrets that married people keep from each other that border on the level of a trip to Las Vegas. Personally, I can't stand the idea of it, but at this point, it all feels like it is far beyond our control. This will be the situation where Marcia gets the real details from Lailah, and I am just relegated to being her "man" and not her best friend. Likewise, this is where Akil will get an ear full, where I would have normally confided most of this stuff to Lailah directly.

My finger hovers over the screen of my phone as I consider whether I should make any phone calls at all, whether it's to Lailah or Jasmine. What I really want to do is hem up that motherfucker Langston in a corner and whip his ass for even thinking that he should intrude on my space like that. Seriously, what kind of punk motherfucker would call up some other guy's fiancée and ask to take her out on a date? A stupid one.

But when all things are considered, I must be a stupid brotha, too, because I'm the fool who let him.

14

We don't talk the next day or the following day. I am still angry and upset, and Lailah is still blaming me for this breakdown in communication. I want to drive by her house to see what's going on over there, but I am much too proud to risk having her see me drive around her neighborhood. I keep thinking that she is trying to stall me out. This is basically a staring contest, and I don't want to be the one to flinch first.

I consider the possibility of just calling Marcia, who has interceding on our behalf before. But what sense does that make? Will we have to call Marcia to fix problems for us when we are married? I need to just get over myself and call her.

So I do.

"Hey," I say, when she answers the phone.

"Hey." Now her voice is as listless as mine was the other night.

"You busy?"

"No."

"Wanna talk?"

"Oh, so now you want to talk."

I know she's being smart, but it doesn't matter, because we need to squash this situation one way or the other. "Yes, I do."

"Okay. Then talk."

"I was hoping we could talk face to face."

"Well, I will come over there then."

"Why can't I come to your house?"

"Because everything that we do is over here."

There is a part of me that is starting to think that she is trying to conceal something from me, but I quickly shake those thoughts away. I have to keep in mind what the objective of our talking is: to make things better, not worse.

"Have you eaten?" I ask.

"Not yet. I had glass of juice earlier. Why? Do you want to go out and get something to eat?"

I laugh. "No. Not even. I was hoping that you would let me cook for you."

I can feel her mood lightening over the phone, and I can sense that we are part of the way out of the woods.

"Okay. I'm about to leave out in the next five minutes. Try not to burn anything before I get there," she jokes.

When we get off of the phone, I feel slightly better about the situation, if only because we are able to talk to each other without the deep-seated animosity. I still feel the anger bubbling beneath the surface, but I breathe deeply, knowing that I am going to have an elastic mind to stretch to her level of dealing with things.

I walk into the kitchen and look in the refrigerator. Thank goodness there is some produce in there. I crack open the freezer part of the unit and take out some chicken breasts. Within minutes, I am sautéing green peppers, yellow onions, zucchini, and squash in a nonstick skillet with a few drops of extra virgin olive oil. In a separate skillet, I am cooking the chicken that I have seasoned with various herbs, salt, and pepper. On a third eye of the stove, I am boiling brown rice. A few broccoli crowns sit off to the side. I will steam them last.

By the time Lailah arrives, I am just setting the small table in my kitchen. Because I drank up the champagne two days ago, I have no choice but to fill the glasses with apple juice. When she comes through the door, the first thing she comments on is the delicious smell of the food. She greets me with a kiss and a very long, deep hug. Being in her arms again makes me feel as though I have really been tripping too hard over the past few days. I want to believe everything that she told me and curse myself for assuming that this sweet angel would ever do anything that would put our love in jeopardy. But it is not easy to do that. No. There are still many things we need to discuss to get over this hump.

But dinner first.

As we sit at the kitchen table, enjoying our meal, we keep the conversation light. I am afraid that if I pop the seal on what I really want to talk about at this exact moment, I will ruin my appetite and possibly hers, too. Instead, I listen to her talk about how things are going with the wedding plans and how she and Marcia will be trying on wedding dresses this week-end. The way that she talks so effortlessly about the wedding would suggest that there is no real issue be-tween us that needs resolving. For a second this angers me, because I have had trouble sleeping, but it seems like she has been getting a good night's sleep the entire time. I hold my tongue and just nod where I am supposed to nod, knowing that once we have cleaned our plates, I plan on shifting gears immediately.

"I love you," she says out of nowhere.

"I love you, too."

"And I'm sorry."

I find that I can't even look at her. When I am finally able to face her, I ask, "Did you know how worried I was about you—about us?"

"I was okay, and as far as you and I are concerned, we will always be okay."

"It didn't feel like that the other night. It felt like you had just completely decided to disrespect our relationship. I mean, who the hell goes out for six hours with their ex while their fiancé sits at home waiting for them? I felt like such a fucking fool!"

She leans forward. "Dizzy, I know you're mad. I get that. But don't think for a second I'm going to just sit here and let you raise your voice at me and cuss at me. I don't play that game."

I soften my voice. "I didn't mean to yell. I'm just hurting, that's all. I had a million thoughts running through my head while you were out and about."

"I told you what happened. If you want, I can tell you where we ate and even ask one of the servers at the restaurant to tell you that I was where I was and did nothing but eat and talk."

"It's not even that serious," I say. "I'm just saying that it was a special day for me, and I had to spend it alone, because of how you handled things."

"Special day?"

"Yeah. This company called Gameland Media is

buying JACOPLEX, and they're buying out my shares."

"Are you cool with that?"

"Am I cool? Yes! I pocket over half a million out of the deal."

Rather than jump up and down like a woman who has just won the lottery, she smiles that deep, rich and dimpled smile of hers, the one that I have always been in love with. "I am so proud of you!"

I don't know how I was expecting her to react, but this calmness is not what I had in mind. She is responding as if she knew that I would always be in a position to catch this kind of windfall, as if I am merely fulfilling a destiny that she had always known I would fulfill.

"Thank you," I say. "But I have to be honest with you. It's all still bittersweet."

"I can understand how that might be bittersweet, especially if you are no longer working with your company."

I shake my head. "No, I'll stay on with the company—for now, at least. I was talking about it being bittersweet that all of the stuff from the other night had to happen on the same day. I had hoped that we could celebrate that evening, and then when I got home and saw you all dressed up—for him—I just totally lost it."

"I'm so sorry. I didn't know."

"I know. But that still doesn't ease the pain."

We sit quietly for a moment.

"Well, was it worth it?" I ask.

"What?"

"The dinner."

"I told you that it was over with him a long time ago."

"But I'm just asking if you got the closure that you needed."

"I'm beyond closure with Langston. He's engaged to some Ethiopian model and preparing to move to Paris."

I chuckle sarcastically. "I wonder if he told his fiancée that he was meeting with his ex-girlfriend for dinner."

"In fact, he did. That's pretty much most of what we did talk about, the two of you."

"I guess I should feel grateful then."

"I'm not asking you to feel any kind of way."

I take a long sip of apple juice and clear my throat. "Well, since everyone seems to be dealing with closure issues, does that apply to me as well?"

"What do you mean?"

"I want to know if I get to go out with my ex-girlfriend to gain closure, too."

"What are you talking about?"

"Closure. That's what we are talking about, right? Closure? I figure if all of you can purge your souls, then I should be able to do the same."

She looks at me strangely for a moment, as if I have told her that I secretly have a third testicle. "I didn't know that you had an interest in going out with one of your exes."

"Well, you never asked."

The words come fast and hard, and I can immediately tell that I have cut her with my words and that I have cut her deep.

I start to back peddle when I see the hurt look in her eyes. "I didn't mean it like that. I was saying that

I should be able to make sure all of my past is completely behind me, too."

My words don't sound any better, but I don't know how they possibly could. The situation I am asking her for is borderline absurd—but it's no more absurd than what she had the nerve to ask of me, especially while we were out doing a wedding planning activity. I have to stand firm on this or I will always feel like the situation is hanging over my head.

"So you want to hurt me because I accidentally hurt you?"

"No. I just want to do what you did, for the same reason that you did."

"Then why are you just now bringing this up? Why didn't you bring this up when I mentioned Langston?"

"I was processing everything. I didn't want to be vindictive."

"So you're not being vindictive now?"

I shake my head. "That's not what I am trying to do."

As I watch Lailah, I start to feel really bad. She looks like she is on the verge of tears, and I realize that I am the only one to blame for this. What makes matters worse is seeing her eyes frozen in sadness makes me realize just how much this woman must really love me, and in that love I know in my heart that everything that she said about her dinner with Langston is true. But I also see in her eyes that she feels that she could lose me to another woman, and that pain and fear is next to unbearable. I could be wrong about all of this, but her look is telling me that I am right.

"You know what?" she finally says. "You are a grown man. You can do whatever you want. If you are doing this because you feel that you have to do it for the greater good of our relationship, I will just have to understand—whether I like it or not. I owe you that, at least. But if you're doing this to get even with me, then I will have to tell you that that is not the best way for us to start a life together. I want to be able to not only trust you, but be able to trust why you do the things you do. I want to know that it is about our marriage and not about your feelings."

"If I do it, it will be for our relationship."

Lailah wipes her eyes. "I trust you."

I walk over and embrace her, and as her face dampens my shirt, I feel that I have already betrayed that trust.

15

———

The idea to launch a start-up is something that Akil has been tossing around for a while now. Even while we were deep in our gaming projects with JACOPLEX, he would say things like, "If we went out on our own, we could do a lot more radical stuff. We are not changing gaming right now, but we could if we were set free to do our own thing." I thought the idea was cool, but I imagined that there would not come an immediate point in time where I had to seriously consider that as an option. Even with the payday that we have coming to us, the reality is that we will be expendable six months after the acquisition goes through. In other words, we will be unemployed.

Now as Akil brings up his favorite non-female related topic outside of work, it is taking on a whole new meaning. He is basically suggesting that we take the buyout and just give a six-month notice that we will be leaving Gameland Media. It is a humongous step, though. I have never run a business before, and the thought of being an entrepreneur is very daunting. The only thing that makes me believe that I might be able to do it is the fact that my cousin J did the exact same thing when he left Wall Street to start a record store in Harlem with his best friend, Cool. Even still, the idea of stepping out on my own scares me shitless.

Akil asked two other people, Michael Dukes and Billy Lancaster, to join this new group of his, but I was the only one he asked who worked at JA-COPLEX. In this new company, I would in theory continue writing the story lines, designing the visual look and feel of the game's universe, and, from what Akil is suggesting, do some of the vocal talent for the game—which I have to admit is extremely cool and a definite deal sweetener.

Michael would be there for marketing purposes, as well as other operational needs, and Billy would serve as a software engineer, since he is already working as a consultant for a few tech companies. The fact that Akil was able to lure either of these two guys to work on a start up company is a minor, but noteworthy, accomplishment in and of itself.

Another minor observation is that both Michael and Billy are white, which gives our core unit not only a diversity of ideas, but a diversity of cultural components as well, and I dig that. I am more comfortable working in very diverse environments, which is something that I loved about New York, but don't see as much of in Atlanta, in spite of their cheesy and untruthful moniker of being the city that is too busy to hate. I will not call that statement an out right lie, but I will say that it is far from the first thing that comes to mind when I think of the city where I live.

I have yet to give Akil an answer, a definite one

anyway, to his invitation to get in on the ground floor, but in all honesty, it would be difficult to tell him no, especially since I am the primary writer and illustrator of this pieced together collective.

Even as Akil continues waxing poetic on a future where we get to live out our dreams of launching a tech company from the proverbial garage, I have trouble focusing on any of this. My thoughts are largely dominated by Lailah and the conversation we had about our exes. Truthfully, it is all a slippery slope. If we are not careful, we could easily paint ourselves into a corner where we are asking about the number of former lovers that each of us have had and any other shit that would tip the scale in favor of unproductive information for a spouse to have rolling around in his or her head later on. Relationships are already hard enough as it is—even without you having to stir unnecessary shit into it.

For now, Akil will have to wait—just until I can sort through the immediate things vying for my attention. When that dust settles, I will be game for considering anything that could take my talents to an even higher level.

&

THINGS ARE STILTED BETWEEN LAILAH AND ME in the days that lead up to my meeting with Jasmine. What seems to be the issue, as far as I can tell, is that she has fixed it in her mind that her situation with Langston is somehow different than my situation with Jasmine. She is quick to point out that Jasmine lives in Atlanta, so that presents a lingering issue that Langston's brief reception did not have. "I don't want to be at the grocery store and wind up getting into with that girl," she said. She even went on to add that, because I had moved back to Atlanta already and we were bosom buddies, she was privy to a few of the details of my relationship with Jasmine, and those few details that she was aware of made her suspicious of any motives that Jasmine would have for wanting to see me now.

Granted, Lailah might have a few points, but I could have argued a number of points about her decision to meet up with Langston. First, she had been in a relationship with that dude for a while. To me —or any guy, for that matter—that basically translates into the fact that there was a lot of sexual activity going on. In fact, she was with Langston much longer than we have been together romantically, so I know he has seen a side of her that I have yet to see or may never see, depending on how things evolve. Those details hang over my head like loose chandeliers. But I'm beginning to believe that this will be one of those things that we will just have to agree to disagree on. The issue now is whether she can handle my being in a reciprocal situation. So far she has been pretty shaky, but I know that it will all balance out in the end.

One difference between the meeting that Jasmine and I are about to have is that I opted to make this a luncheon type of thing, as opposed to a dinner where we would be stuck waiting two hours to get a table at some snazzy restaurant in Buckhead. And I am not even dressing up, just throwing on a t-shirt and some jeans. If anything, these details should have mattered to Lailah, but apparently they don't.

Now, as I sit out in front of a deli in Smyrna

waiting for Jasmine to arrive, I wonder if I should call Lailah to put her mind at ease and let her know that she is in my thoughts and my heart, but then I remember sitting up those six hours feeling like a damn fool waiting on her to call while she was out with Langston. I figure that she will be okay. I am sure that she will survive, just as I did.

Jasmine pulls up in her BMW 325 looking like she would never in her life associate herself with the likes of a plain ass Negro like myself. The irony is now that I will have the means to get a car like hers or one far more luxurious, I am not even interested. If anything, I want to see if I can reach the magical number of 400,000 on the odometer of my Jeep Wrangler before I break down and buy, you guessed it, another Jeep Wrangler.

"Hey, Dizzy," Jasmine says, walking up to me and wrapping her arms around me. She hugs me like a friend—but a friend with history. The touch lingers a second longer than it would have if I was just someone she knew from school. She is wearing a sleeveless pink blouse and a pair of tiny khaki shorts so that her long, toned legs are accentuated. Her hair is done in a way that suggests that she could afford to get real Indian hair rather than the traditional yak from the Korean shop in West End. She looks as if she could be famous by the way she moves, her small Gucci handbag tucked neatly under her arm, the matching Gucci shades resting on the hair above her forehead. She looks good! Painfully so.

I order a sandwich; she orders a salad. We make small talk for a while, before she asks, "So why are you getting married now? What happened to change the nature of you guys' relationship?"

I consider telling her the truth, but then I wonder if she even deserves to know the truth of it all. The last thing I would want is to open my relationship with Lailah up to any feedback and possible criticisms from a woman who has no shortage of opinions on things. Instead, I respond, "We just realized that we were the ones for whom we had been waiting."

"June Jordan poem, right?"

"I think so. Still it is true."

"You know, I kind of wondered if maybe we would get back together down the road."

"I offered you a chance for us to have a real relationship together, and you were the one who rejected it."

She smiles, picking over her salad. "You know me and relationships."

"I never did understand that about you. You would be monogamous and spend all of your time with me, but you didn't want to be my girl."

"I didn't want to feel like I belonged to you. Hell, I don't want to belong to anyone for that matter. Why can't two people just spend time together and enjoy each other for what it is without creating all of these artificial labels."

I sigh. "They are not artificial or arbitrary. They are just people's ways of affirming their feelings and making it known to others that they stand behind those feelings."

"Sounds unnecessary to me. Why should I be concerned about what people outside of my situation think about my situation? That's a bad way to live life—pleasing others. I mean, you knew how I felt about you without me having to make some bold and pointless declaration."

"How do you know? I'm no mind reader."

"You know because I spent all of my time trying to please you and keep you satisfied."

"You make that sound like it was all one-sided," I say.

She smiles. "Well, we kept each other satisfied. Everything was cool. But then you went and jinxed it."

"I don't see it that way, but that is all in past now and there's no point in waking up that sleeping bear."

She laughs. "Whatever."

"What?"

"Whatever," she repeats. "You don't want to wake up sleep bears? Right. Why did you want to get together with me if you didn't want to take a trip down Memory Lane?"

In that moment I see the entire span of our relationship, and I realize at that moment that we were never in love. It was always about sex. We had built up a powerful emotional connection simply based on one emotion: lust. Sex was the way we communicated. It was the way that we expressed our thoughts to each other. It was the heart and soul of who we were as a couple. All of the conversations that we had were simply preludes to sex. I once heard a magazine publisher make the statement that to editors, ads are the things that go between their stories, but to ad people, editorial content is the stuff that fits neatly between the ads. The epiphany is mind blowing. We were never in a relationship that had any real gravitas. We just had a lot of really good sex, and I guess if you could hang your hat on that for the rest of your life, then cool. But I was not that kind of person. There apparently was no way that Jasmine and I would ever have survived in any kind of relationship of any depth. Our relationship was bound to end eventually. The fact that it did when it did is just the result of something naturally running its course.

I can't even be mad at Jasmine for that. It was what it was for the time that it lasted, and I can tell that she is in no way apologetic about any of the failings of our situation, nor should she be. As I consider this, I realize that her coming to see me would be built more around what connection that we did once have together, and that is when I realize just the magnitude of the mistake I made in coming here. If we defined ourselves on sex and I was not willing to consider that, then we were just wasting each other's time.

There is still a part of me that is attracted to her, but when I think about how Lailah is the epitome of beauty, sexiness, intelligence, humor, and loyalty and how I have always known this, I am immediately ashamed of the fact that I allowed myself to go through with this situation and sit up here in public with this woman, who while very sexy, is not the woman who can do a damn bit of anything for me at this point in my life, save mess the entire thing up.

"It's been good seeing you," I offer, as I rise from the table.

"What? Where are you going?"

"I really shouldn't even be here right now," I say, feeling like a bad imitation of Eddie Murphy when he leaves Robin Givens alone on the bed in her thong so he can head home to Halle Berry. But this is not *Boomerang*. It's my life, and it's important for me to bring things down a few notches and refocus on what is really important to me: Lailah.

"Whatever," Jasmine adds, as if she is totally unfazed.

"We both know that this is not the move. You deserve more," I say. "And I actually have more. Take care."

She doesn't even look up as I walk away, and while I want to think that I might have made her feel bad with my sudden departure, I have a gut feeling that Jasmine does not care one way or the other. Life has always gone on for her, and I have never been the reason that she has changed the way that she has done things. She walked away from me once before, so I know a second time would require even less thought.

As I pull off, she has already initiated a conversation with another guy at a neighboring table.

Jasmine, I think, laughing to myself. I hope she finds what she is really looking for out there, but I can't be concerned about that now. I need to get to Lailah as fast as I can.

&

WHEN I GET TO LAILAH'S HOUSE I FIND THAT she's not there. I call her, and when she doesn't answer, I leave a short message letting her know that I want her to come over tonight. By the time I pull into the parking lot in front of my apartment, I am reeling with thoughts of Lailah and how lucky I am that she is the woman I will be marrying. I am already thinking of picking up a bottle of champagne and some rose petals, because I want to do something really nice and special tonight. I am pulling out all of the stops. This will definitely be a night that she will never forget. I don't just want her to have orgasms tonight; I want her to be unable to walk at all. To put it in the words of Wanda Sykes, I am going to lick that woman cross-eyed.

When I get to the door, I see an envelope taped to it. The penmanship is familiar. In fact, it looks a lot like Lailah's penmanship. I quickly pull it down, my heart overflowing with joy. Stepping into the apartment I start reading the letter, and within the first two sentences, I find that I have to sit down to stabilize myself.

Dear Dizzy,

This is hard for me to say. I have been doing a lot of thinking about our relationship, and I am not sure that we are ready to get married. Don't get me wrong. I do love you. And I do want to marry you. But I feel like we might be rushing things a bit. This whole thing just kind of came out of thin air, and I am not really sure how to take all of it. We have been friends for our entire lives, and that is what we are good at. This new thing that we have is nice, but it is new.

I am not used to being jealous or having you be jealous. Granted, I probably should have dealt with the Langston situation differently, I did not expect for you to automatically assume the worst of me. I thought you loved me and trusted me enough to know that I would never do anything to hurt you or what we have. Your friendship is all that has ever mattered to me, and the fact that you assumed that none of that mattered to me hurt me more than anything else.

As far as you going out with your ex to spite me, I expected better. I know that you would have never even gone out with her if I had not met up with Langston. That makes me wonder how you would deal with situations in the future when I do something that you do not like. Will you always feel the need to one up me or make sure that I feel what you have felt, although I did not intend for you to feel that way?

I thought that I could handle all of this, but I realize that I just can't. Not right now. And I think we would have known this about ourselves if we had taken things much slower. I have no doubt that you love me and that you want to be with me. I have never questioned your love, and I have never questioned the love that I have for you, but I think there is still some room for what we have with each other to mature. And when the time is right, we should continue our trip to the altar. But right now, maybe we should take a little time to ourselves to see what it is that we are really trying to do and what voids we are really seeking to fill in our individual lives.

Love,

Lailah

I stare at the letter for a solid minute, my eyes unblinking, before I reread it two more times, stopping only when the tears have blurred my eyes to the point that I can no longer see.

16

After three attempts at calling her, I realize that she will probably not answer my calls for a while. I then consider hopping back in my car and driving to her house and waiting her out. In my opinion, we need to be talking this out, not avoiding each other. The temptation is strong to hop in my Jeep, but I fight the urge, mainly because I don't want to further complicate the issue by being that guy who just can't get it through his thick skull that the woman needs space (although I guess I am that guy anyway). I would hate for her to be hiding over at Marcia's place having some conversation where my acts are deemed "crazy" or "creepy." Not that I would think Marcia would feed this, but I don't know what Lailah is going to tell her about my meeting with Jasmine.

On another level, I am more than a bit disappointed. I might have hated every last second of the six hours that I waited for her to come home off of her date with Langston, but I did not bail the hell out of this relationship. That was not even an option to me. The fact that she could ask for space so quickly after I went on my lunch date, not even waiting to hear back from me, makes all of this feel even more one-sided. Maybe I was the bigger sucker. Maybe I should have been more adamant about her not going out on her date, but instead I gave her the benefit of the doubt—like friends are supposed to do. Did she cut me any slack? No. Is she out somewhere thinking of herself as self-righteous, as if she is the victim in all of this? Probably. All I have is her letter, the last word for now on all matters dealing with us.

I am stunned.

I don't even know what the next move is. Do I wait her out, at least until we can have a true heart-to-heart talk and let cooler heads prevail? Or do I call my parents and tell them that the wedding is off for now? I can hardly admit such a thing to myself, so I am adamant that I not admit that to anyone else. There is a part of me that still feels that I can salvage things. I refuse to believe that we are so far gone that talking can't fix things. The greatest irony though? I left the lunch date headed directly to be with her. And that move actually was more than she made an effort to do for me.

Unable to stand being in my apartment any longer, I hop in my Jeep and drive out to Interstate 285, a belt around the city. I figure I will just ride the belt until I have a clearer head, and then go from there.

As I exit onto the highway, my phone starts ringing. My stomach tightens as I check the caller display and realize that it is my father, not Lailah. I consider letting the call go directly to voicemail, but I want so badly to talk to someone who might be able to understand more of what is going on than I do.

"Hey, Dad," I say. My voice is dry and weak, and in that moment I realize that all of the thinking that I had done did not involve my speaking at all.

"Hey, Dizzy!" my father says, his voice jovial and full of life. "How is my favorite son?"

"I'm your only son, Dad."

"That doesn't mean that you can't still be my favorite," he says, laughing.

"I'm surviving."

"Are you okay?"

"Not really."

Against my better judgment I cave in and tell Dad what happened. And I tell him everything. I go all the way back to the day we were putting together the registry and Lailah brought up Langston. It takes me nearly fifteen minutes to get out the entire story, my actions included, and the entire time my father just listens patiently, so patiently that a few times I have to ask if he is still on the phone, because I can't tell if he is listening or if I have lost my phone connection with him. When I finish, my father says, "Don't give up hope. Just give her some time and space."

His words are simple and do nothing to bring me any peace. "How long? I can't take this!"

"Whether you want to or not, you will take it— especially if you love her. People from your generation are lacking something that we had back in my day: patience. I don't know if it is all of this Facebook/Twitter stuff that has you guys desperate for immediate feedback or what. Sometimes you have to sit and be inconvenienced with not knowing the answer to a question about something. It's only been a few hours, and you have jumped to a million conclusions."

"Dad, you don't understand," I say interrupting him. "Things now days are different than they were in your day."

"Maybe. But I doubt it. You told me what the letter said, and if my memory serves me correctly, she did not cancel your engagement. She just asked for some time to sort a few things out."

I exhale into the phone. "It means the same thing, though."

"What makes you say that? We have both known Lailah her entire life. When has she ever said anything but what she really meant? That girl has never held back her true feelings on anything. You have to remember that this is Lailah, not one of those other women you have dated. She doesn't have an incentive to be vague with you."

I consider what my father is saying, but I'm still not convinced.

"I feel like I'm losing her. For all I know, she may already be lost to me," I say.

"So you had a fight. Fights happen. I can't think of any married couples who haven't broken some plates over the years. That's how you learn how a person is in a marriage, and that is usually different than they are outside of a marriage. What I'm trying to tell you is that there are always growing pains when two people start setting up a life together. There are things you learn about each other that you might have never known, and you have to understand that all of that is a part of the process of being one."

"We were doing so well before all of this."

My father laughs. "Then you were overdue. That is how you know what your relationship is made of, the mettle, if you will. How you handle the situations where you disagree on things is how you ultimately define your marriage. Do you go running for the hills every time something goes wrong or do you ride it out and find a way to make peace? Seems like you could both stand to learn a little bit about that."

Listening to my father, I am not comforted by his words at all, but I know that there is probably a great deal of truth in them. I want to make peace with Lailah, but I just don't know how to do that— not with her taking this space from me.

"Did Mom ever need space from you after you guys had a falling out?" I ask.

"Everyone needs space from time to time. If you don't get anything else from what I am telling you, get this much: it is hard, very hard, to mend situations if you are constantly all up under each other. Grown people need space sometimes. If every waking moment two people have are spent all up under each other, then when do they get a chance to miss each other and to learn how to have some sense of independence in their marriage. Now don't get me wrong. You need to be of one accord, especially in your public front, but at home you have to be two people who have your own thoughts. That part doesn't change. What does change, however, is that you understand that you are on the same team and that you are a part of a championship team as long as the two of you are together."

I love it when my father uses sports metaphors, but hearing this one in the context of relationships causes me to pause. Up until this moment I had never considered Lailah and I a team, but when I think about it, we have been a team for a very long time. The only things that have changed are our positions.

"So what do I do now?" I ask.

"Stop playing tennis against each other."

"What?"

"You guys are playing against each other when you should be playing doubles as teammates."

I shake my head. I have to remind myself that my father loves tennis, a sport that I played briefly in high school but have not played in years. For a moment I think that he has switched metaphors on me, but then I realize that the championship team he was talking about earlier was a doubles championship team and not football or basketball. With my father, it was tennis all along.

"What exactly do you mean?" I ask, trying to catch up with his thinking.

"Seems to me that every times she scores a point on you, you feel the need to answer with a point of your own. She goes 15 - love, and you come back 15 - 15, and then she goes 30 - 15, and you guys go back and forth, but what you do not understand is that it doesn't matter who wins, because if either of you beats the other then you both lose. It's not 30 - 15; it's really 30 - love. The only thing is that you guys are love, not 30."

His words have my eyes wide open now. The metaphor is as heavy as a greasy piece of Church's fried chicken, but I understand where he's coming from. That's when I remember the cross stitched picture that used to sit in the foyer of our house when I was growing up. The image of two tennis racquets crossing each other to form an "X" comes to my mind.

"Tennis is the only game where love means nothing," I say, remembering the words beneath the intersecting racquets.

"That's what they say," my father says. "But the key to that statement is the 'only in tennis' part. Everywhere else, love means everything, and that is what you have to remember with Lailah. Love is all the two of you have. Hell, it should be the only thing that the two of you show toward each other, whether it is just friendship or more. So stop playing tennis against each other. Your love is supposed to mean something, if not to anyone else, at least to the two of you."

"I see what you're saying," I respond.

"You know, I was not going to say anything about this, especially since you are a grown ass man and can make up your own mind about things, but your mother and I were a little surprised about how quickly you guys put this marriage in motion. It's like the two of you skipped the dating stage altogether. Back in the day we would have to court for a while before we started even thinking about what you guys are planning on doing. Courting gave you not only a chance to get to know each other better, but it also helped you to not make rash decisions. If you had strong feelings about someone, it gave you a chance to get that newness off the relationship before you made any permanent decisions. You guys seem to have just skipped that part altogether and went head long into a situation that put you on the immediate path to the altar."

At this point, I can't even be angry at anything that he is saying. This is the first time that my father has told me his thoughts about what Lailah and I were planning, and hearing his words is sobering.

He continues, "Robert and I thought that there was a possibility that the two of you would one day hook up, but that was not the reason that we named you guys Dominique and Dominic."

"Why did you?" I ask. I had been told various things throughout the years and the one that made the most sense to me was that we were born on the same day, just like twins. I was content to accept that rationale, but now my father has brought up the subject, so my curiosity has returned.

"I know your mother and I always told you that it was because the two of you were born on the same day, but that is only part of the thing. The other part is that we wanted the two of you to be close throughout life. Robert and I grew up together, and we wanted our children to have, at the very minimum, a friendship that spanned their lives. The fact that you were a boy and Lailah was a girl only opened up the possibility that the two of you might one day be more. The funny thing is that it took you guys thirty years to flip the script on us old folks."

We laugh, and for the first time this evening I have felt a burden lifted from my chest. I know that Lailah is still upset with me, but knowing that we have always been connected to each other, by design, I feel that anything that we are confronting now is small in comparison to the thirty years we have survived as friends.

"Dad, do you think that everything will work

out and that Lailah and I will be able to get past all of this?"

"Dizzy, it really doesn't matter what I think or what your mother thinks or even what Lailah's parents think. It only matters what the two of you think. We gave your friendship our best shot. The rest of this, engagement and all, is purely up to the two of you."

"Thanks, Dad."

"No problem. I love you."

"I love you, too."

When I hang up the phone, I start heading back to my apartment. I have an idea of what I need to do now. I just hope that what I think I know about my friendship with Lailah is as real as I believe it is.

17

___

On the night that Lailah and I agreed to marry each other, all those years ago in her dorm room at Georgia State University, two things came out: one, that I wanted to one day marry Lailah, and two, that she would only marry me if it was her last resort. Those kinds of details tend to escape your mind when you are romanticizing your past. It never occurred to me to replay the entire conversation before launching into my plans to propose to her. In other words, I was only concerned with what I wanted, not what she might have wanted. In fact, this entire situation might just be the result of me pushing her into an area that she might not have originally wanted to be.

Of course, I want to believe that all of that has changed—or at least that it was changing. The love I feel from her is genuine. I feel it not only in her words or when she touches me, but also when she wraps her legs around me and pulls me into the warmth of her body. I can feel it in the movement of her tongue as she kisses me. There is nothing in the way that she physically relates to me that leads me to believe that she is doing something reluctantly, but lest I forget, what is physical does not always reflect the total being of someone. As single thirty year olds, our desires for physical affection are not lost on me. The question is whether or not an engagement and all that is involved in not just a wedding, but a life together as husband and wife, is too much for either of us right now. After all, should two people be bound for life based off of a pact that the two of them made when they were still fresh out of their teenage years? For the longest, I wanted to believe that, but now I am not so sure.

What I do know is that she is so important to me that I don't want to lose anything that we have together, whether it's friendship or intimacy. And if I am being completely truthful with myself, I want to marry her more than anything in the world, and I would do it in a phone booth in New York City during the middle of rush hour, if it meant that we could be together forever. But that is what I want. I can't begin to be so presumptuous as to know what it is that Lailah wants, and the last thing I would want her to do is something that she is not ready to do, pact or not.

Other than talking to my father, I have not told anyone of the road bump Lailah and I are experiencing. I don't know if she has told anyone either, so I sit quietly, not ready to make any public announcements to anyone about a change of date or postponement of the wedding. More than anything, I just want to talk to Lailah and hear anything that she wants to say. What she wants will largely determine what we do, and I have resigned myself to be as flexible to her wishes as possible.

Admittedly, there is still a part of me that believes that she was wrong to go out with Langston, but if I cling to that feeling, we will never be able to move forward. Sure, my reaction might have been spiteful in some ways, but that, too, has to be left in the past, that is if we want to move forward with our relationship.

I pick up my phone and call her again. I get her voicemail, but I decide against leaving another message. By now, I have left at least five of them, and I figure that if she wanted to call me, then she would have done so by now. My phone has not rang, so my guess is that we have not turned the corner on what is bothering her just yet. Still, there is a part of me that is starting to wonder if it is possible that we will ever turn that corner. And the thought of that stagnant future for us scares me. In fact, it is my greatest fear when it comes to us. Losing her. That is what has haunted me since all of this began. Never has such a feeling been so tangible as it is now, and I have not figured out how to process it. This is the thing over which I have no control. I am completely at her mercy.

I hold the phone in my hands, briefly considering whether or not I should call her again, but I quickly decide against it. This is something I will just have to wait out. Still, the idea of driving over to her house gives me some small hope. I have to squash this immediately though. I am not going to stalk her just because I am missing her like crazy. After all, I don't want to be the impossible, insufferable dude that smothers his woman because of the burden of his emotions.

I put the phone down, walk into my bedroom,

and fling myself across my bed, closing my eyes until my fatigue gels with sleep and I drift off.

§

THE SALE OF JACOPLEX GOES THROUGH without so much as a hitch, and we are told that the disbursements will occur within thirty days. They even bring in a few financial consultants to talk to us so that we understand the tax consequences of such a transaction and what options we would have if we wanted to minimize the government pillaging off nearly half of the amount. They also remind us that we have a six month contract going forward as independent contractors, which means that we no longer have benefits like health and dental insurance. I guess they figure that we will be able to afford that with our buyouts. We are also reminded that Gameland Media might very well hire some of the JACOPLEX team on when the contract period expires. I feel my chances are decent of still having a job with them at that point, but I am not so vain as to believe that a company as large as Gameland Media would not be able to replace me with someone or some group within its existing team. There are clearly no guarantees here.

And when I think about Akil's offer to come and start a new company with him, I realize that there are hardly any guarantees there either. If anything, I will still be without health and dental insurance. There is also a chance that it might be a minute before I actually get paid much money. The bottom line is that I have no guarantees either way.

Duvall tells us that we will continue working out

of our current office building until the independent contractor period expires. He has not told us what he plans on doing at that point, but I would be surprised if he went to work at Gameland Media. He is independently wealthy now, and he is young enough that he will probably want to do a number of other things, besides heading up a division and working under a CEO who is even more outrageous than Duvall ever was. Word is that Gameland Media's CEO, Greg Dermott, is such an asshole that he sends out his nicer, and much easier on the eye, COO, Mrs. Bishop, to do most of the face-to-face meetings with those outside of the company.

Greg Dermott does not intimidate me, but at the same time, I am not sure I want to continue down the path I am on. Everything just seems uncertain at this point. I don't know where I stand with Lailah, and I don't know where I stand with my career either, but sooner or later, I will have to ascertain my answers on both.

Akil asks to meet with me for lunch, and I agree, although I am not sure what I want to tell him about Lailah and me just yet. Thankfully, his mind is in other places when we sit down to eat.

"So are you in on this new venture or what? I need to know something soon, because I have set up a meeting with a few money people, and they are going to want to know just who our team is going to include. People won't come up off the ducketts, unless they know what they are paying for."

I nod. I understand where he is coming from and why there is a sense of urgency to his words this time. I have been stringing him along for a while, I know. It was not intentional, but things were just so hectic with the wedding plans that I felt I could afford to push back my response a little while. Well, I have bought more time than I actually had, and now Akil needs to know something.

What's the worst that could happen, I tell myself. Even if I have to dust off my resume in the future and go interview for a job if everything fails, I will be all the better for venturing out and trying something new. I will have a chance to do a job that I am defining as I go along. It is a rare opportunity to be able to pick up so much experience at one time. Plus, Akil is focused and is every bit the hard worker that I am. I seriously doubt that the two of us together would result in the company failing.

"I'm in," I finally say.

Akil's reaches across the table and hugs me so hard that I have a flashback to Mr. Landfair's last bear hug in Daily, Mississippi. I am both comforted and immediately nervous. I have a million and one unanswered questions swirling around in my head, but I know that I will learn the answers as the days progress.

I wonder if it will be the same way with Lailah, though. It has been several days, and we have still not spoken to each other. I start to tell Akil about what's going on, but I do not. He even asks about when we will go do the fittings for the tuxes, but I just shrug and offer, "Soon," returning his attention to our new business venture. "So what will be the name of this new company?" I ask.

"I am still playing around with some different names, but I keep coming back to Dantes Games."

"Why Dantes Games?"

Akil smiles. "My favorite book is The Count of

Monte Cristo by Alexandre Dumas. The main character's name is Edmond Dantes."

I shrug my shoulders. "And how does that connect to what we will be doing?"

"Have you read the book?" he asks. "You majored in English in college, right?"

"Yeah, I can't say that I got around to reading that one."

"It's an excellent book," he offers.

"Yeah, I'm sure that it is, but you're still not answering my question."

"I was just about to get to that. Check this out. Edmond Dantes is framed for a crime that he didn't commit, just because this dude had the hots for his woman. Anyway, Dantes is sent to this really jacked up prison and forced to serve out his term there indefinitely. While in there, he hooks up with this old dude who tells him about this treasure hidden out there in the world. The old dude starts to train him and make him into a protégé, but the old dude ends up dying before the two to them can break out of prison. Well, Dantes decides to break out of prison on his own and goes off to find the treasure. Once he finds it, he creates a whole new persona and enters town as the Count of Monte Cristo, and no one knows who he is, because he has a whole different swagger about himself since all of this stuff went down. Anyway, he plots his revenge and ends up getting the dude who set him up at the beginning."

Even after this rambling synopsis, I still don't know what any of this has to do with naming the company, unless it is just because he likes the character in the story. "So that's it?" I ask.

"Well, what I was thinking is that we, as a company, are reinventing ourselves to come back and take over the game."

"But are we doing this out of revenge?"

"Nope. We are doing it one better. We are doing it out of necessity."

I nod, finally understanding Akil's motivations. "Well, that's all you had to say."

18

———

I have not attempted to call Lailah again for several days, although each day that passes by feels as if we are causing even more irreparable damage. Never in our lives have we consciously avoided each other for this long. Even during that episode that occurred during our junior year in high school, Lailah never left me feeling as if she had completely abandoned our friendship. Now I am beginning to wonder if she even cares, if her actions are really justified by what has happened so far.

Maybe it is just like she warned me, though. Without me being there to hear her vent her thoughts, I have forced her to confide what she would have automatically confided in me to another person altogether. My guess is that Marcia is the one who is getting an earful at this point. But why hasn't Marcia stepped in to try to fix all of this like she did after my proposal? Maybe she disagrees with my going out with Jasmine, too. I wouldn't be surprised if she did. Still thirty years of friendship should trump all of that. It's not like I cheated on her or anything. If anything, I have worked to show that

Lailah will never have to question my feelings for her.

I scan the numbers in my phone, hoping to find Marcia's, and when I don't find it, I silently curse myself for accidentally deleting it. Only a guy would find himself in this type of situation, because a woman is too smart to be left in this awkward position of being unable to contact anyone in her lover's inner circle.

With Lailah not answering her phone, me not even having Marcia's phone number, and my refusal to drive by Lailah's house, giving off the illusion of stalking her, I am left with very few choices. I can either wait her out completely, hoping that she will end this estrangement sooner than later.

Or there is one other thing I can do!

As the idea fills my head, I immediately wonder why it took me so long to even think of it. I must have been so devastated that I couldn't see the most obvious solution. I immediately run back to my bedroom and lift Lailah's letter for me from my dresser. I take it into the room that functions as my office space and begin to read it again. While the act of doing this stings me a bit, I know that it is necessary. Once I finish, I lie it down next to my laptop. I pace the room for a few minutes, collecting my thoughts, before I take a seat at the desk, pull the laptop up to me, and begin typing.

It starts out simply at first, but the longer I sit there, the longer I realize that this might be my only chance to communicate my true thoughts to her without her trying to completely dodge me. I doubt, in my heart, that she is so cold as to not read a letter that I have written to her, especially if I am not there to watch her attempt to ignore it. She has left me little choice than to contact her using the exact same method of communication that she used with me. I am just hoping that she had not expected me to do that all along, because if she did, I totally missed that memo. But knowing Lailah, she was probably preferring that method of communication to begin with. After all, she is a writer of literature, and as she often says, "Characters have to have a legitimate reason to do whatever the action is that the author attributes to them. They can't just do things for the hell of it. Motivation is important."

Staring at the laptop screen in front of me, I realize that my motivation is clear: I want my fiancée back—in the worst way—but if I can't have her back, I simply want the friendship that she has shared with me all of these years to remain in tact so that I can at least feel the wholeness of her presence in my life again.

My fingers move slowly at first, as I search for the right words to illustrate my feelings. I labor through the first paragraph, stopping often to reread sentences and tweak them to make sure that I am paying the same level of attention to the words that I know she had when she wrote me her letter. The farther along I get, the faster my fingers begin to move, until I can see my thoughts jumping eagerly from my fingertips with the click of each key. The screen begins to fill with words, and for the first time since I got her letter, I begin to feel something buzzing deep within my chest: hope. I can't say that it is hope that everything will work itself out, although I know I want that desperately. I think that it is more of the fact that I am finally able to unload certain things from my mind so that she will at least know my thoughts and feelings. Being unable to transfer these thoughts to her and having to hold all of my thoughts hostage with no form of relief available left me feeling even worse than just being floored by the contents of her letter. It was as if she was saying, "You can sit and dwell on my thoughts, but you can not offer me your own." And while I could not tell it at first, I was beginning to become poisoned with the inability for me to release my thoughts to her. I had become toxic—until now.

Once I finish typing the words of my letter to her, I stare at the screen for a moment and sigh in relief. There they are. My thoughts. They fill the screen and are no longer clogging my thoughts, tripping over each other and giving off the illusion of being much more amplified than they really are. I was a victim to them before I sat down. Now I have liberated them onto the screen. I quickly save the draft, because all I need is for some freakish act of nature to cause these thoughts that I have so desperately culled from the recesses of my brain to vanish like a fart in the wind. Then I think of Lailah's embarrassment at learning that she pooted in her sleep. I laugh to myself, feeling a tug in my chest like gravity pulling me back down to earth and the current situation that lies before me.

I reread the letter on the my laptop again two more times before printing it out and lying it down on my desk, right next to Lailah's handwritten letter. I immediately wonder if I should try to write my letter out, too. The thought comes quickly before scattering away when I realize that it is Lailah who has the beautiful penmanship, not me. My chicken scratch would not make much for a pleasant visual. Plus, her being able to understand my words clearly is the main thing. Anything that would risk creating a barrier in communication has to be cut out of the equation immediately, and my penmanship would definitely fall into that category.

I turn my letter to her face down on the desk and then turn it back over, imagining that I am Lailah seeing the words on the page for the first time. I reread the letter a final time.

Dear Lailah,

My heart is heavy as I write this, because I have missed you so much in the past few days. Not being able to see your beautiful smile or touch your soft hand or hold you in my embrace until I dissolve completely in the warmth of your body has left me out of sorts. My heart remains every bit yours since the day we came to know each other, but my mind is restless with wondering how long this estrangement will last.

I have read your letter so many times that I have committed entire passages to memory, and I understand why you wrote it. I get where you are coming from, and I value and appreciate your thoughts. Please know that it was not my purpose to make you feel uncomfortable. And you, of all people, do not have worry about anyone else competing for my attention—bar none (including Janet Jacme lol!!!). You have, are, and will always be the most beautiful woman in the world to me. The one thing that I have going for me that I can brag on without question is the fact that I knew this from the time we realized that we were even in this world together. Yes, together. Because with you in my life, I have never been alone, nor would I ever want to be.

I could rattle off all of the smooth movie lines that

you have heard throughout the years if you need an illustration of what you mean to me:

*"You're my air. I can't breathe without you." —
Marcus Graham in* Boomerang

"You're my rib."—Jody in Baby Boy

"You had me at hello." Dorothy Boyd in Jerry
Maguire

*Well, you get where I am coming from. The bottom
line is that I not only love you with all of my heart; I
need you just as much. "You complete me." (Yeah, I
know I am stretching that movie out a bit here.) Still,
it's true. It's all true. You are all of these things to me.*

*While I know that this might not mean much to
you at this point, I am sorry for everything that I have
done that has made you question our relationship. I
think that we have both done things that we would
have done differently if given a second chance, and I
know I definitely did not need to go out on my five-
minute luncheon with Jasmine. I knew that from the
moment I sat down. What you and I have is so special
that I feel as if being in the presence of another woman
for longer than a few seconds is a waste of my time. She
could never be you, nor did I expect her to be. Deep
down, I know I should not have even bothered to see
her again, but when you told me about Langston, I was
hurt. I tried to play it cool because I thought that was
what you expected me to do, and I guess if I had just
been honest with you about my feeling jealous, none of
this would have unfolded the way that it has.*

*You said in your letter that maybe we could have
avoided this problem if we had not rushed into to this
engagement, but I disagree. We are engaged because we
are in love with each other, and we want to spend our
lives together for the rest of our days, not because we are*

trying to put ourselves into a category where we never make mistakes with each other again. That is impossible. We are just as bound to make mistakes as we are to have days that are challenging. That is life. But what has made all of that bearable, at least up until this point, is that we knew that we had the other person there to help kiss those sore spots and to make them feel better.

I can't promise you a perfect life, but I can promise you a life where you will never have to feel unloved or unappreciated. I can promise you a life where your laughter will be my favorite song. I can promise you a life where you will never have to go a day without knowing that you are the queen of my heart. And I can promise you, God willing, that we will still be side by side on the porch of our house at the age of ninety, staring off into the sunset, fingers interlocked, still in love.

That is what I want for us. And this temporary snafu is not enough for me to feel that we cannot be all of those things to each other—now.

Yes, this situation is a bit unexpected. I get that. But it does not mean that our love and commitment to each other is any less true. The way we went about it is just different, not better or worse. Just different. And different is what has always defined our relationship to each other, whether we were friends or lovers. You are my other half. We are the only ones who get the "gooney goo goos" of our relationship, and I love that about us. We can have a house full of love and children who grow up in that type of love and carry it with them into their own relationships. That is us. I understand this. You understand this. Our parents even understand this. We were made for each other, and in the words of Stevie Wonder, "I was made to love you."

I would apologize for rambling in this letter for so long, but I can't. I miss talking to my best friend, and this is my way of being true to what we have. I am not the writer that you are, but my motivations can never be questioned. I am as easy to read as a Dr. Seuss book. My theme is and has always been simple: I love you.

With all of my heart,
Dominic "Dizzy" Parker

I fold up the letter and slide into an envelope. It is far from eloquent and definitely is not a masterpiece by any stretch of the imagination, but it is how I feel, and having put it all down on paper makes me feel a bit freer.

I consider whether to mail the letter or just hold it until she makes contact with me. After all, I am still trying to respect her space, although inside it's killing me. I begin combing through my room looking for a book of stamps when my phone rings.

"Hello?"

"Dizzy?"

"Yes? May I ask who's speaking?"

I don't recognize the number on my phone, but there's clearly a tone of familiarity in it.

"This is Dorothy Landfair."

Why in the world is Lailah's mother calling me? I immediately assume that something really bad has happened to Lailah.

"Is Lailah okay?"

"She'll be all right."

I don't know what to make of the comment, so I inquire further.

"She told me about what you guys have been going through," she says.

"Oh. Mrs. Landfair, let me tell you that I never intended to hurt Lailah in any way. I love her so much."

"I know."

"I've been trying to get in touch with her, but she told me that she needs some space."

"I know," Mrs. Landfair responds again. "She's just a little stressed out about all of this, but I wanted to call you and tell you a few things so you might better understand where she is coming from."

"Okay," I say, unsure if I'm going to be told off by another member of her family.

"Lailah really loves you. I know this. I also know that she's afraid of being hurt. Robert and I know that you would never hurt her, though. Even Lailah knows this. I know she really wants to see you and talk things through, but she's afraid. Being in a few bad relationships can do that to someone."

"I understand."

"I've been trying to get her to communicate with you, but I figure you might be better at that than I am."

"So you're saying I should go over to her house?"

"I'm not going to tell you what to do, because that's up to you, but I can tell you that she wants to see you as much as you want to see her."

I consider exactly what Mrs. Landfair is saying and immediately stop looking for stamps.

"Mrs. Landfair?"

"Yes."

"Why call me and tell me any of this?"

I hear a soft chuckle in her voice before she responds. "Your mother and I had been talking to Lailah about the wedding planning, and as soon as this came up, we both knew it was just a case of cold feet. I told your mother I'd call you to see how you were handling things on your end."

All of this is blowing my mind. I try to wrap my mind around our mothers conspiring to save our relationship, and for the first time in a while, I feel that all is not hopeless at this point.

"Thank you so much for calling, Mrs. Landfair."

"You don't have to thank me. Just make my daughter happy."

"I will do everything I can to make that happen," I respond.

After we say our goodbyes, I grab the letter I wrote and hop in my car.

In the drive over, my heart beats rapidly and I can feel my stomach tensing. Every stretch of road feels as if I am moving slower than slow. I wish that I could just fly to her house, but this time I have alone in the car with this letter is the moment I must be in. It is the moment where I do not know what will happen. It is the moment where anything is still possible, where I could be moments from reconciling with the woman I love or moments from losing her altogether, regardless of what our mother's might think. There is a part of me that believes that we will be able to remain friends in spite of what happens, but I already know that that's not all I want. I want so much more for us than that.

It is in this moment that I exit the interstate and take a detour. There's a stop I have to make before I go see Lailah. If this will be my last chance, I want to go all out.

19

———

I see Lailah's car in the driveway as I pull up, and I realize that I have never been this nervous in my entire life. There are no other vehicles in her driveway or in front of her house, and a part of me is relieved that she is alone. I don't know what I would have done had I seen another car there, other than turn around and leave. My only hope, should I have stumbled up on that situation, is that it would have been Marcia and not Langston. I shake my head to clear the thought of that. Clearly, I'm tripping. There is nothing between them. I know this—or I should know it—but that does not stop my mind from wondering.

I approach the door, slowly, feeling the weight of each step I take up the driveway and onto the footpath that leads to her front door. I take a deep breath before ringing her doorbell.

In the seconds between my ringing the door bell and hearing her opening it from the other side, I live a lifetime.

"Hi, Dizzy," she says.

I am flooded with relief just to hear her say my

name. I immediately open my arms to embrace her, and she quickly closes the space between us by wrapping me in her thin arms.

I miss the feel of her, and I inhale the scent of her wild raspberry lotion, enjoying the tickle of her curly hair brushing against the side of my face. I am at home—finally.

"I missed you so much," I immediately say, not wanting to let her go.

"I missed you, too."

I hold her a beat longer, and she allows me to.

A million questions flood my head, and I don't know where to begin. Instead, I simply say the obvious. "I'm sorry."

She nods, her face solemn. "Yeah, I'm sorry, too."

When she says this, I reach for her again and she allows me to hold her, but I can tell that there is still something beneath the surface that she wants to tell me, so I hold my breath cautiously.

Lailah leads me into the den and takes a seat on the end of the couch so that I am seated in the middle of it. As she looks at me, I notice that she is wearing an Ellison-Wright t-shirt that I gave her a few years ago while raiding the bookstore for paraphernalia during one of my trips down from New York. That makes me smile, and I hope that her wearing that shirt is a deliberate attempt to keep me close to her thoughts.

She looks as if she is contemplating what to say, which is totally uncharacteristic of her, and I can feel the mood in the room shift, as if the air is being quietly sucked out. I reach in my pocket and quickly produce the letter that I spent the morning writing. I hand it to her quietly.

She stares at it for a moment as if trying to figure out what it is. Then she takes it from my hand. There is nothing enthusiastic in her actions, nothing that screams a curiosity at what I have written. She places the sealed envelope on her lap and begins to twiddle her fingers. I wait for her to read the letter, but she doesn't.

"Dizzy," she starts. "I have been doing a lot of thinking over the past few days."

I stand up from the couch. "Okay. Before you go any farther, I need you to read that letter."

She looks at it curiously, but doesn't make any attempt to open it. "We need to talk about a few things."

I feel the hope in my veins beginning to drain. I start to pace the floor, as I feel my face warming. "I agree," I finally say. "But please read my letter first."

Her eyes move from one side of the room to the other, as she considers this. With a deliberate cautiousness, she opens the envelope and removes the paper inside.

For the next several minutes I watch her, unable to look away. Her expression remains unchanged the entire time, and I know immediately that I have lost her. And that feeling floors me. I stop pacing and stand there with my heart beating slowly and powerfully in my chest. My stomach feels as if it has slid down into my legs and hangs heavily at my calves. This is the one thing that I have feared more than anything for as long as I can remember.

I sit down next to Lailah. Not because I want to, but because I have to.

Her eyes are still on the page, although I know that she has already finished reading the letter. I want to say something to her, but I know that she has to be the one to speak first now. She knows my thoughts at this point, and that was all I could hope for when I wrote the letter.

When she finally opens her mouth, I stop breathing.

"I appreciate your letter."

I nod.

"I have been doing a lot of thinking about what we are doing, and I thought these last few days would help me to figure that out. But I'm not sure that it has," she says.

"That's not such a bad thing, though. Right? I mean, we can't know the answer to every question."

"Maybe not, but all of this is so big. So much!"

"Maybe. Love is like that, though."

"So you still want to do this, I'm guessing," she says.

"More than anything in the world."

"But there is so much that you don't know about me. Just because we have been friends for forever does not mean that we know how to be together in a relationship."

"True, but we can learn all of this stuff as we go along. I love you enough to get to know you in every way that you will allow me."

"But I might need more time to get to know you the way I would need to know you in order for me to get some of these questions out of my head."

"What kind of questions do you have?"

"I don't know. Questions, ya know?"

"Talk to me, baby."

"You know. Like will you always try to get even with me if you think I am doing something wrong to you? Will you naturally assume that I have the worst of intentions when I do something? I need to know that you won't just trip out on me and do something—just because."

"I am promising you now that I will not."

"But you can't really promise me that."

"Why not?" I ask.

"Because you can't know what the future will hold. Only time would tell if this was a fluke or if you really would handle the situation differently."

"Lailah, all I have is my word. You have to believe me when I tell you that I only want you to be happy. I can't sit here and tell you that we will never argue or have fights, though. That's not real. Our parents can't even say that they have never had their own problems with coping with each other's peccadilloes. That's just a part of life, but in all honesty, I don't even have to tell you any of this, because you already know this. What I need for you to do is to really tell me what's on your mind and not hide behind this argument."

"I am not hiding," she responds, but based upon the weakness of her words, I can tell that she is not using much passion to hold it up.

"Please. Just let me know what is really on your mind. I'm still your best friend."

"I want to believe that."

"You can take that to the bank and cash it for a million bucks. That is how certified my words are."

She considers this for a moment and then stands up. Now she is pacing the room, her movements almost identical to my movements from a few minutes earlier. I can tell she is sorting through the different ways of making her comments.

"Lailah, just say it. I can take it."

"Okay," she finally says. "I need to know that we are not just settling for each other because the situation is convenient. I guess that is what crossed my mind when I went out with Langston, and it was the first thing I thought about when you told me that you wanted to go out with Jasmine. I figure that if we would be so willing to go out with people that we used to date, people that we spent much more time getting to know intimately, then maybe we're not ready to be with each other for the long haul. At least, not yet."

I consider her words. I know in my heart how I feel about her, but what she is doing is telling me that she has not been as sure about all of this as I have been. We can talk all day long about Jasmine, but this is not about her. It is about Langston or some dude who has yet to even enter the picture. I'm not totally sure, but what it feels like she is telling me is that she doesn't know if I am the best that she can do. The thought stings to the core.

"As much as I wish that I could convince you of how much I love you, I know that you will only accept that when you are ready to. And I know that you will only be comfortable with the idea of being married to me when you have reconciled how you really feel about me. I can't force that part. I have to just let you figure out that part yourself. But, real talk, I can't tell you anything about my feelings that you don't already know. Even if you decide you don't want to follow through with our engagement, I will always love you. I don't know how to do anything else—and I don't want to know how to do anything else. But I can't do all of this by myself. You have to want it as much and as badly as I do."

Lailah nods, her eyes glassy, but unyielding.

"Can I ask you a question?" I say.

She nods again.

"Do you love me?"

"Yes," she responds. Her voice is soft, but firm.

"Can you see us together?"

"Yes."

"Can you see yourself spending the rest of your life with me?"

For a moment she doesn't say anything.

"La, I'm asking you a simple question. Can you see yourself with me for the rest of our days?"

Her head moves slowly at first, up and down, and then more enthusiastically. "Yes, I can."

"I'm sorry. I couldn't hear you," I lie.

"Yes, I can."

I chuckle.

"What?" she asks, her face full and glowing.

"You sound like you're campaigning for President Obama."

"What do you mean?"

"Yes, I can! Yes, we can!"

"Boy, you so stupid!"

"But I love you more than words can say."

She hugs me, and I sear this moment into my memory: the feeling of her body wrapped tightly against mine, the sweet smell of her skin, the tickle of her hair against my cheek, all of it.

"So will you marry me?" I ask.

"Yes."

"I mean now, not three years from now."

"Yes, Dizzy," she responds, playfully hitting my shoulder.

"I want you to be sure. I want this to be what you really want, because you're all that I want."

She lowers her head, blushing. "It feels funny telling you this, but I have always been trying to find a guy like you, and now I realize that I didn't want a guy *like* you. I wanted *you*." She laughs to herself. "I can't believe I just said that aloud. You know, sometimes you think things, but you keep them to yourself."

I nod, unable to conceal my smile.

"Now you're here, and I have these feelings for you, and I just don't want to ever lose you," she continues.

"You will never lose me. We're a package deal. We came into this world together, and I want to be with you as long as God will allow."

She kisses me gently at first, then more passionately. It's the first kiss that we have shared in days, and I realize that I have been aching for her touch.

We continue kissing for one interminable moment, before finally ending in a tender embrace.

"Oh," I say, stepping back slightly. "I forgot. I have something for you."

I retrieve the package from my pocket and hand it to her.

"What is it?" she asks.

I reach for her left hand and pull it to my lips. I kiss it softly and gently remove the ring that she is still wearing. I reach over and open the box, taking out the new 1.5-carat solitaire that I had been admiring from earlier. I kneel down in front her, still holding her hand.

"I love you, and I always will. And I would be honored to have you as my wife."

She allows me to slide the ring onto her finger.

"Yes!" she says, looking the ring for the first time. Her smile is even wider than before. For a moment she stands there staring at it, before she lifts it to her face for a closer view. It takes me a moment to notice the tears streaming down her cheeks. "It's so beautiful!"

"Just like you."

I take the other ring, the costume one, and start to slide it into my front pocket, but she stops me.

"Can I keep that one, too?"

"Sure," I say, handing it back to her.

"Dizzy, we're really going to do this, huh?"

"Yeah," I say, chuckling. "We are. Can you believe it?"

"I have to pinch myself."

"No you don't. This is the reality that we've always wanted for ourselves."

She smiles. "I love you so much."

"I love you, too."

As we kiss, we slowly dissolve into each other.

One together in love, at last.

20

EPILOGUE

$\mathcal{A}$kil doesn't complain about the cranberry vest and tie that he and the other groomsmen will have to wear. In fact, he helps me to pick it out. My tux is nearly identical, except that my vest and tie are white. I will have to wait three more months to see how my tux looks against Lailah's dress, but just knowing that it is going to happen is good enough for me.

Dantes Games, LLC is now official. We have even started pre-production on a new game that I have been playing around with for a while. It is a simple puzzle game that requires the player to assemble a group of clues and then solve a moving puzzle board. It is definitely a safe bet for a first game, but nothing spectacular. Our next project will be a bit more involved, though. Akil just wanted to make sure that we had something going to market before our independent contractor contracts expire with Gameland Media. One of the benefits of not being an actual legitimate employee right now is that we do not have to sign the same type of non-compete agreement as other employees, although we do have to respect the confidentiality policy of the company.

I imagine that most of my future will be up in the air and full of unpredictability, but I am cool with that. If anything, it will guarantee that when I turn thirty-one, I will have a few new adventures to look forward to.

STANDING OUTSIDE OF ST. PETER C.M.E. Church with two months to go before our wedding, Lailah and I are cuddling while leaning against my Jeep Wrangler. I can't help but to think about when we were much younger, possibly six or seven, and we used to run around this church (it was much smaller back then, without the add-on of a cavernous fellowship hall). We would chase each other after church, playing "Tag" and screaming at each other "You're it!" like we had no good sense. All the while our parents stood around socializing with other adults from the church. We had to stay busy and active to keep from getting bored. Plus, we were hungry. Even on first Sundays when we had communion, and those small little crackers and packets of grape juice only further amplified our hunger. We had fun though, sneaking each other pieces of candy during the pastor's sermon.

I wish I could say that when we entered high school we were much more focused, but we weren't any more focused than when we were children, often passing notes to each other during the service, making our usual comments on the selections of our tone deaf choir. Now as we lean against the side of the church, it occurs to me that our getting married here is probably the only serious thing that we will have ever done here.

"Lots of memories here," I say, stroking Lailah's hair softly.

She chuckles under her breath. "I guess we had to grow up sooner or later."

"Yeah," I respond. "You are probably right."

The parking lot is still gravel, after all of these years, and while the church looks different, it still feels the same.

"Remember Pastor Brown?"

"How could I forget?" I say, laughing. "He always called us frick and frack."

"Yeah, and he would always mispronounce words in the Bible."

"I remember that. I think I remember him reading out of the New Testament one time saying something like, 'Jesus walked through the garden of Big Word, and he Big Word. Then the Big Word became the Big Word.'"

We laugh hard, remembering how Pastor Brown wrestled with pronouncing words that had more than six letters in them. It probably wasn't supposed to be funny, but we couldn't help but laugh. In a church where many of the members of the congregation had college degrees, it was expected that whichever pastor the bishops assigned us would be able to at least read publicly from the Bible without butchering the King's English.

"Be serious now," I say, trying to stop laughing. "Did you think that we would ever be here, getting married?"

"It might have crossed my mind when we were

little, since we used to play like we were married all the time anyway. I guess there was a part of me that wondered if it would ever happen or even if it could happen."

"I feel you. I knew from the first time that I put that Cracker Jack ring on your finger that I wanted to be with you."

"You were only six then. You couldn't have possibly known what you wanted back then."

"Yes, I could. And I did. And I still do. With you, it has always been easy. Loving you has just come naturally for me."

Lailah lifts her head to me and kisses me. As our lips touch, I feel a warmth come over me. Everything in this moment feels so right, and I find myself unable to stop wishing for our wedding day to come sooner.

"It is a good thing that you never stopped loving me," Lailah says, nestling her head against my neck."

"Why do you say that?"

"Because I would have hated to be alone on that one."

I smile. "Never that, Lailah. Never that."

"I guess we should go back inside and finish the last of our pre-marital counseling sessions."

Our fingers interlock, and I glance at her left hand. The diamond on the ring glints in the afternoon sun.

As we enter the side of the church and head for Pastor Edwards's office (he has now been at the church for two annual conferences), Lailah squeezes my hand excitedly.

Just two short months away from now, I tell myself, and I find myself unable to stop smiling.

OTHER BOOKS BY RAN WALKER

B-Sides and Remixes

30 Love: A Novel

Mojo's Guitar: A Novel/ (Il était une fois Morris Jones)

Afro Nerd in Love: A Novella

The Keys of My Soul: A Novel

The Race of Races: A Novel

The Illest: A Novella

Bessie, Bop, or Bach: Collected Stories

Four Floors (with Sabin Prentis)

Black Hand Side: Stories

White Pages: A Novel

She Lives in My Lap

Reverb

Work-In-Progress

Daykeeper

Most of My Heroes Don't Appear On No Stamps

Portable Black Magic

ACKNOWLEDGMENTS

I would like to thank my family (nuclear, extended, and in-laws) for their support. I would also like to thank Sabin Duncan, Kyr Mack, Phill Branch, Van G. Garrett, Nsayel Mputubwele, Kathryn DeShields, and The Whittington family for their encouragement of this project. Also, I would like to give a special thanks to a true friend and survivor, my "little sister," Brandi Ray.

For all of you who have read and supported my work up to this point, thank you. Your feedback and enthusiastic word-of-mouth are truly appreciated, and I will be forever grateful.

Last, but by no means least, I would like to thank my beautiful wife, Lauren, for her love and encouragement, and my lovely daughter, Zoë, who continues to amaze and inspire me.

ABOUT THE AUTHOR

Ran Walker is the author of seventeen books. He has written novels, novellas, short stories, flash fiction, microfiction, and poetry. His short stories, flash fiction, microfiction, and poetry have appeared in a variety of anthologies and journals. Prior to becoming a writer and educator, he worked in magazine publishing and practiced law in Mississippi.

He is the winner of the 2019 National Indie Author of the Year Award (selected by judges from *Library Journal, Publisher's Weekly*, IngramSpark, St. Martin's Press, and *Writer's Digest*), the 2019 Black Caucus of the American Library Association Best Fiction Ebook Award, and the 2018 Virginia Indie Author Project Award for Adult Fiction. He is also the recipient of both a 2005 Mississippi Arts Commission/NEA artist grant and a 2006 artist mini-grant. He served as an Artist-in-Residence with the Mississippi Arts Commission in 2006. Additionally, he is a past participant in the Hurston-Wright Writers Week Workshop and is the recipient of a fellowship from the Callaloo Writers Workshop.

His novel *Mojo's Guitar* was translated by renowned French translator Philippe Loubat-Delranc and published in April 2015 by Éditions Autrement as *Il était une fois Morris Jones*. The novel was recently republished in May of 2019 as a part of Éditions Autrement's "Les Grands Romans" collection.

His first collection of poetry, *Most of My Heroes Don't Appear On No Stamps: Kwansabas*, will be published in August of 2019 by The University of Hell Press, based out of Portland, Oregon.

Ran is a graduate of Morehouse College (BA in English), Pace University (MS in Publishing), and George Washington University Law School (JD). He also has a Certificate in Publishing from New York University and has done graduate work in English at Mississippi State University.

Ran is an Assistant Professor of English and Creative Writing at Hampton University and lives in Virginia with his wife and much better half, Lauren, and his amazing little rockstar daughter, Zoë.